EARTH BOUND

EARTH BOUND

DRAGON OF SHADOW AND AIR BOOK FOUR

JESS MOUNTIFIELD

DISRUPTIVE IMAGINATION

Dedication:

To any woman who was ever confident about something they were good at. And had it mistaken for arrogance.

LMBPN Publishing supports the right to free expression and the value of copyright. The purpose of copyright is to encourage writers and artists to produce the creative works that enrich our culture.

The distribution of this book without permission is a theft of the author's intellectual property. If you would like permission to use material from the book (other than for review purposes), please contact support@lmbpn.com. Thank you for your support of the author's rights.

LMBPN Publishing
PMB 196, 2540 South Maryland Pkwy
Las Vegas, NV 89109

Version 1.02 December 2021
eBook ISBN: 978-1-64971-849-5
Print ISBN: 978-1-64971-850-1

CHAPTER ONE

As I landed on the roof of the dojo with Zephyr, I grinned. We'd just flown back from the beach, something that hadn't been possible a month earlier, and it was still daylight.

"Aella, Zephyr, there you two are," Erlan said, getting up from a sofa just inside the small rooftop shack we'd made. It was a semi-permanent fixture, several small rooms having been created to allow all the people living in the building some privacy or quiet time away from everyone else if they needed it.

Not everyone could fly away at a moment's notice to the beach or go relax away from the pressures and demands of the building. But after spending months on the run and cooped up inside, I was only so sympathetic.

"What's up?" I asked as Newton came scurrying over and climbed up Zephyr. The two creatures were firm friends, and it had always helped ease the relationship between Erlan and me. I'd found the other elf's presence a little awkward. I'd been worried I'd lost a friend to him when Newton the fire salamander had bonded with him and become a smaller part of my own life.

I couldn't really complain, however. Zephyr was a dragon and not only a huge part of my life, but our bond ran deep and we were both descended from some of the most powerful mythicals in our history books.

"Minsheng asked us both to be in the dojo at three. Said he wanted to get our training started early today," Erlan said, looking toward the door into the large warehouse.

The building housed the Bronze Dragon Dojo. It had been turned into that by a friend of mine despite me owning the building. That wasn't what bothered me, however. I couldn't remember Minsheng asking me to be early at all.

"Come on then," I replied. "We'd best not keep him waiting any longer."

Hurrying down the steps, I heard the rest of them thunder behind. I'd gotten so used to using my powers to control the air by default that I often had to concentrate not to run and move faster than those around me. But Zephyr was never far away.

We'd had the building modified in the last few weeks. The stairwell up to the roof was now far larger and Zephyr could fit on it just fine.

It wouldn't be big enough forever; almost nothing was. Zephyr was going to keep getting bigger for a while, but his growth had slowed, and I was hoping to persuade the organization to help fund us adding several floors to the warehouse.

Minsheng stood waiting for us in one corner of the warehouse's main floor. It was a spacious area that Erlan and I often practiced in, along with our bonded mythicals.

There weren't many props set up there, but that didn't stop us from practicing all sorts of uses for our powers. I controlled the air by reaching out to it somehow and connecting on a basic level. It then moved at my whim.

For almost half a year, I'd been training to control it, and apparently I was a natural. I think it helped that I'd been learning from people who knew what they were doing. Erlan had been learning to control fire far longer, but he struggled with his lessons, having barely been able to achieve anything until he'd bonded with Newton.

It was confirmation of something Minsheng had long suspected. Bonding with mythicals made both parties stronger.

Instead of being angry we were late, Minsheng was still reading through something on his laptop.

"Okay," he said when he saw us. "I think I've finally deciphered the next few pages in this manual from the Sanctuary. It's clear we were trying to train in the wrong way."

I wasn't sure what he was talking about as my training had already surpassed the knowledge of most of the content of his book, but he'd been working on something with Erlan the day before.

"You do need the catalyst," Minsheng said. "But you shouldn't need a fuel source beyond that."

Definitely not me.

Still interesting, however, Zephyr replied even though I'd not been talking directly to him. Our bond also gave us a telepathic link.

"Great," Erlan said, having not heard anything but Minsheng's explanation. "Let's get started."

"Well, there is one thing we should discuss first," Minsheng replied. "As you're both aware, the organization has been paying me to look out for elves who have woken their magic and possibly bonded with mythicals. They've been taking reports on the progress of both of you for some time now, and I've been Aella's Shishou for the whole time."

I lifted my eyebrows, suspecting where this was going. Minsheng had been badgering the organization to make a decision on Erlan for some time.

"They've agreed that you are making good progress here, and officially added you to my list of potential wards. If you'll accept, Erlan, I'd like to formally request to be your Shishou as well as Aella's. It would allow me access to more resources to teach you both and hopefully make it easier for us to work out ways to combine your powers."

"Sweet," Erlan said, quoting one of the movies he'd recently watched. "I'd be honored."

Erlan had spent the early part of his life in the Sanctuary, and I'd been giving him a catch-up education on everything important to the average American young adult. He appeared to be enjoying it. And it helped me unwind too.

I waited for Minsheng to talk about what that meant for Erlan, zoning out as I looked at the nearby cabinet. Minsheng and I kept a lot of our gear in this one cabinet at the edge of the dojo, and it contained some interesting items we'd picked up along the way, including a couple of orbs that guided us to the Sanctuary.

One was in perfect condition and was still lit up, trying to guide me somewhere east and a little south. The other I couldn't fully see. This second one occupied my thoughts if I let it. I'd been given it by courier, and it was broken. Not only that, it was covered in blood. Dried blood.

Although I didn't know whose, Minsheng had sent some samples off to the organization to try to get it tested. He'd not entirely explained why, but the organization had told us we'd get results soon.

With the orb, I'd also received a note. It had informed me something wasn't over. I could only assume it was the war I'd been embroiled in, and it was from Jacobs, the shadowy man I knew had been ordering Crawley and Knox to hunt down mythicals in LA and nearby locations.

I had no idea where he was now and what he was up to, but so far everything had been peaceful.

"We still don't have any more info," Minsheng said as he came closer. I glanced back, noticing Erlan and Newton both starting little fires in a safe section of the floor, surrounded by water in case something went wrong.

"I'm not sure we're going to. But I intend to stay on my guard. And train," I replied.

"Of course. How is it going, using your powers to help Zephyr fly faster?"

"It was going really well until we went so fast I started to slip off his back," I replied.

"Hmmm." Minsheng put his hand to his chin and looked thoughtful. "Could you also form a better slip-stream around yourself so you aren't hit so badly by the wind?"

I tilted my head to the side for a moment, considering it.

"Maybe," I replied, imagining the few times I'd thickened the air and held it still so well it had formed a sort of wall. Could I do something like that?

"Want to try to practice it? I can use a fan to simulate wind, and you can see if you can redirect it by holding air still around yourself."

I grinned, grateful Minsheng could think so fast. Behind me I heard Zephyr sigh.

"Don't worry, big fella," Minsheng added. "I've got plenty for you to do to train as well."

As long as it's not another kind of boring assault course, I heard Zephyr say in my head. I had to ignore him and not smile at his annoyance. It wouldn't help to pressure Minsheng. The first few assault courses that Minsheng had made had been difficult for Zephyr, but he was so large and strong now that there weren't many problems that he couldn't just ram straight into.

His genetic memories gave him another advantage on top of that. Anything that he could remember his ancestors doing was easier for him to do or learn himself. And he had a fair few memories now.

"You're flying well, but not silently or as efficiently as you could. While Aella can speed you up, it makes it easier if you can fly with as little effort as possible."

"So you want me to practice flying?" Zephyr asked, his disdain clear. Although Zephyr was completely capable of speaking in English, he often chose not to bother, keeping his communication to the telepathic bond.

"I want you to practice lifting off without blowing out a

few candles," Minsheng said a moment later, almost grinning to himself.

It was my turn to chuckle. Genetic memories didn't make up for practice when it came to doing something difficult naturally and well. He knew how to do what was in his memories, but not the whys or nuances in the best way to do something. Sometimes he simply knew that something was possible without having tried it himself.

Once Minsheng had him practicing and Erlan and Newton had moved on to the fire salamander spitting acid into some kind of cup, Minsheng and I finally set up my fan.

At first I felt very silly standing in front of a fan and concentrating on it in a way an outside observer might mistake for who knew what. The fan was stationary and I could feel it pushing at my hair and clothes.

Trying to relax and focus, I took a couple of deep breaths. Somehow I had to put everything else out of my head for a bit and just try to learn. In some ways that was often the hardest part of all the training. Beginning it.

Once I started it was easy to keep trying things for a while. To lose myself in the task, but starting in the first place... There were always plenty of other things I wanted to do more than train.

In truth, I was never far from exhausted, and it was beginning to get to me. I'd been training or fighting for months. And now I had TV appearances in the mix. While now and then I could sneak away with Zephyr, most of the time I was needed.

Now, I had to focus again, however. Pushing the thoughts away, I reached for the air around me with my magic. I found I was already connected to a lot of it, the habit of reaching for it now so ingrained in so many settings that I did it automatically. I connected with more, however, bringing the air in tighter around me and holding it steady.

Almost immediately the breeze from the fan lessened and I could feel it grow fainter on my skin. Concentrating, I continued to refine the process, but I could still feel it a little bit, no matter what I did.

Then I remembered what Minsheng had said about making myself more streamlined, and instead of just making a harder, more dense pocket of air around my body, I tried to make something wedge-shaped and contoured to help me get the air to flow to either side.

This did the job, and I found myself grinning.

"Succeeded?" Minsheng asked a moment later, looking up from his book again.

"Yup," I replied, feeling smug. Minsheng didn't respond but got up and flicked the fan onto a higher setting. Immediately I could feel it again and had to try to work out how to reduce the blast or deflect it even more efficiently.

It was a lot harder to reduce the blast on the next setting up, and it made me angry. I'd managed to stop bullets with walls of air before. Why was this so much harder?

I voiced the question out loud at Minsheng a few minutes later. He thought about it for a moment.

"I'm not entirely sure, but I think it's because air particles are so much smaller and you're stopping it with particles of a similar size. You also often actively stopped bullets by moving the air within your wall toward the bullet."

I nodded. It made sense, but it didn't make me feel any happier about it. In short, Minsheng had made it clear that it was easier to prevent something that was sporadic or large.

But stopping something I couldn't even see properly was another matter entirely. Still, I concentrated. Every application of my powers that I learned would help me become stronger and better.

I'd come back from the visit to the Sanctuary earlier in the year stronger in every way. All the things I'd practiced there enabled me to use my abilities for longer and longer periods without growing so weary.

I also suspected it helped make my bond with Zephyr stronger. Or, at least, something did. Over the months we'd grown bonded more, our awareness of each other and the mental link between us becoming effortless and clear as time had passed.

No sooner had I managed to block out all the air on the second setting of the fan than Minsheng got up again and set it to the third. I growled as he sat back down.

"You've made good progress," Minsheng said. "I thought it would take you a few training sessions to master it on the first setting, let alone work it out on the second too. The similarities between the two barriers must help. You've had some previous experience."

I nodded, not telling Minsheng that I often held a barrier around myself when I was out in public. I didn't put it past Jacobs to have a sniper come after me and try to take me out.

While I wasn't paranoid enough to always wear a Kevlar vest or anything, I was paranoid enough to form protections with my powers. No one else could see those, but I knew they were there.

Blocking air out was simply about making the area denser and pushing back a little. Mostly, anyway.

The magic was still a little strange. I didn't know how come I could do many of the things I did, but I could feel a connection with the air around me, and then I simply had to think and concentrate on what I wanted it to do. The more I did it, the easier it got and the quicker the air obeyed. I'd assumed it was like learning anything else.

CHAPTER TWO

"I need a break," I said, my body beginning to shake from low blood sugar. I'd been trying to block out the third level of the fan for what felt like hours. After I'd beaten the lower two settings so easily I'd been determined to try to beat the most powerful, but the air kept slipping through.

While I sat down at the nearest available soft spot, Minsheng reached into a pocket and pulled out a granola bar with a grin on his face.

"Perfect," I said as I took it. It had become a thing. More than once, I'd pushed myself too hard while training and needed something quick and easy to eat. Minsheng always had one on hand.

Zephyr flopped down beside me a moment later, panting and clearly exhausted as well.

When do we get to go on holiday? he asked. *A real holiday, with palm trees and swimming.*

Good question. But I didn't know you could swim.

I've never tried. Pretty sure it's just like flying but through water instead of air.

I chuckled, getting looks from some of the others before I remembered that they couldn't hear the conversation I was having. Although I was grateful Zephyr could make me laugh, I knew he was only doing it to see if I'd be embarrassed.

It didn't take my mind off the current state of affairs. I thought I'd have still felt safe despite the threat in the message, but instead, I felt like I was in limbo. Was something worse coming? Who knew?

Before I could decide if I wanted to train more or do something else, Daisy came down the stairs carrying a wrapped package. She immediately had everyone's attention, and I grinned.

"Erlan," I said. "You might want to come sit down for a bit and train later."

The elf looked up from the spot he and Newton had been sitting in while they practiced their fire techniques. I'd seen him take a couple of breaks, but his attitude toward training was almost as fierce as mine. He'd only stopped when forced to by the sheer energy required to concentrate for so long, and as soon as he was rested, he got straight back to work.

Now, however, he seemed to happily rush over to us. Minsheng offered him a bar as well, making my smile grow even wider. Seemed I wasn't the only one beginning to like to them.

"What's this?" he asked as Daisy came and put the package on the table.

"Well," she said, "you told us you hadn't ever had a birthday present, and we know it's normally more of a human thing—after all, elves and dwarves and lots of the other races live a good bit longer—but we wanted to get you one. This is from all of us."

"This is a present?" he asked, his eyes going so wide I thought they might pop out of his head.

"Yup, and you can unwrap it however you like. Rip the paper off, tear open one end and slide it out, or see if you can peel the whole thing and preserve the wrapping." I pushed it toward him.

Daisy had wrapped it really well in a bright blue wrapping paper covered in happy birthday messages, cake and party hats—the kind of paper you'd put on a kid's present.

Given the contents, it really amused me.

He started by trying to peel it carefully, but when the paper tore slightly, he went with the flow and pulled it open to reveal a laptop.

"Is this... Can I use this for the internet?" he asked.

I laughed, and several of us nodded. Erlan had taken an interest in all the things he could get on the internet and use a computer for and had kept borrowing Daisy's. Giving him his own had been a simple solution to a couple of problems. It allowed the kid to explore it in his own time.

It also reminded me of another laptop. I still had Crawley's from the agency before Zephyr and I had brought it down. I'd booted it up and looked at it a couple of times, but I'd not got very far or managed to crack the password to log in.

Erlan had tried to help me. He was one of the few people who even knew I'd taken it, but so far, neither of us had managed and the battery had been running low. To make matters worse, I hadn't thought to grab the charger for it when I'd taken it and we didn't have a matching cable to charge it with. Not until now.

Daisy and I helped him open it up and turn it on.

"Can I get on that site you were using earlier? So I can help you with the people you're monitoring," Erlan asked, looking at Daisy.

"The social media stuff? Yeah, I can help you get set up on some of that. I just keep an eye on how people are reacting to Aella and mythicals in general. Put in a good word for us where I can."

"It all helps," I replied. "As long as we don't waste time with trolls."

"There are trolls on social media too?" Erlan's mouth fell open.

Daisy laughed as I shook my head.

"It's a word we use to describe people on the internet who deliberately say misleading and unkind things to make arguments happen and others feel bad about themselves. They feed off the upset it causes."

"Oh, that sounds awful," Erlan said, suddenly looking like he might not want his laptop at all.

I tried to reassure him that most people were nice, even on the internet, while Daisy continued to install what we needed.

"How's everything going?" I asked when she handed it over to Erlan to fill in his details.

"There's still some resistance to the idea that mythicals exist," Daisy replied. "And I think there might still be some agents out there trying to make you look bad, but it's hard to prove it's not real people. A lot are sympathetic or excited. However, quite a few hope to meet Zephyr, and all sorts of people across the globe keep saying they've seen you and him flying."

"We do go out," I replied, more worried about the people who still didn't want to believe in us. We'd been on so many TV shows. Was it so hard to accept that we'd been here for a while in hiding?

"I know, but according to the internet, you were in Tokyo on Monday, Moscow on Tuesday. Somewhere in South Africa on Wednesday morning, and Australia by Wednesday evening. Apparently there's arguments going on about you being in either London or Barcelona by Thursday, but people are sure you were in both places, so..."

I shook my head. It was insane. I'd been in LA since coming back from the Sanctuary. I'd even done all my TV interviews and things like that from LA. Almost all of the studios were here.

"Anyway, I should go help with dinner. We've got everyone in tonight. And then I want to see about getting the top floor expanded officially," Daisy said. "With the mythical family of gnomes who decided to come back after your big interview, we're a little low on living space again."

I sighed and nodded, reaching for Zephyr. There were so many different problems to deal with that I was glad that I didn't have to tackle all of them by myself. I still had to handle a fair amount.

For a few minutes, I helped Erlan get set up on social media while everyone else went and cleaned up the warehouse floor to get ready for the dojo lessons that evening and the mythicals who lived with us to return.

"Does this fit that laptop you stole?" Erlan asked almost

immediately once we were alone with our bonded mythicals. As he spoke, he held up his charger cable.

"Yeah. It should," I replied as he handed it to me.

"Why don't you go get it? We can try to get into the thing again."

I considered saying no. Part of me wanted to be the one who broke into it and found out what had been going on and if there was much more of the agency elsewhere, but I wasn't getting very far.

"All right," I said. "Let's relocate to somewhere a bit less out in the open and see what we can come up with."

Trying not to think about the fact Erlan was still a pretty young elf and I was letting him break the law with me, I led the way to the living area on the top floor and went into the small space I used for storing my belongings.

It took me a moment to dig the laptop out from underneath all my clothes and belongings. I'd deliberately hidden it. There wasn't a lot of privacy or safe places to put anything, so I'd made it look like it wasn't even there.

Then I plugged it in and booted it up, but it brought me to the familiar screen I couldn't get past.

"Needs a username and password," I said. "But I've got nothing to go on."

"There's got to be some way to bypass it and keep all the data on it," he replied.

I lifted an eyebrow, wondering where he'd learned the word data. But as he clicked around his new laptop and started looking for information, I could see he'd been practicing and was familiar with functions and options I couldn't easily find.

"Leave it with me," he said. "I'll let you know if I get into the machine."

Again I considered objecting, but Zephyr nudged me toward the stairs, so I knew he was bored or hungry. There wasn't a lot for Zephyr to do while we were at the warehouse, and I didn't want him to be bored while I poked keys.

What do you think we can do to convince people we exist? I asked Zephyr as we walked back down to the main living area that also doubled up as the changing rooms for the dojo while it was open.

I don't think we can convince everyone without appearing in front of them. Lots of people don't believe in something unless it's right before their eyes, and even then, they like to explain it away. Think of how many people believed I was an animatronic, or a small dog, or all sorts of things before we told them I was actually a dragon.

Zephyr had a good point. We'd hidden him in plain sight more than once. People didn't want to believe in dragons. Especially not ones that had been living on their planet for millennia. It had become my job to convince them.

The others had told us to rest and not worry, that there was plenty of time to let the world know we really existed, but I wasn't so sure. There was so much resistance on social media, and I wouldn't put it past someone like Jacobs to capitalize on it.

Still, there wasn't a lot I could do right now but get stronger. And I'd promised to start teaching one of the dojo classes each week. That meant getting ready to train people.

I hurried down to the dojo, already in suitable clothes. I just had to just stick a gi top on and grab some pads if I was going to need them near the end.

Zephyr found somewhere to watch, but he only kept one eye on us. With the other, he watched the cameras we'd had installed around the building.

That was the other new job the residents had performed on rotation: guard duty. Or security. Keeping the building safe. More than a few times, we'd had mythicals show up at the door hounded by press, thugs, and on one occasion, the police. We gave them a safe place to rest for a moment.

"Got another one," Zephyr said aloud, making me and others jump. It wasn't the end of my lesson, but I motioned for Lyra to take over as I rushed to Zephyr's side to see what he meant.

Chris appeared too, looking over the dragon's other shoulder at the camera feeds. Near the front door was what appeared to be another dwarf, a heavyset male carrying something. He kept looking over his shoulder and then knocked again.

"Let him in," I called and ran toward the front door as quickly as I could, using my abilities to practically fly up the stairs and then through the people milling around until I was going down the stairs on the other side of the building.

Daisy was already at the front door, her hand reaching to open it. The second she touched the handle, I slowed to a normal speed. I tried to keep the full extent of my capabilities to myself until I knew I could trust the newcomers to our place.

There were a few exceptions, but an unexpected dwarf wasn't one of them.

As Daisy opened the door, the dwarf hopped straight through it, almost knocking her over. He caught and righted her before looking around. The moment he spotted me, he sighed and exhaled, the package under his arm proving to be something he'd bought.

"Oh, thank the stars. I've found you, truly found you. Please, you have to help me," he said, his voice coming out in one deep rush.

"Slow down," I replied. "You're safe enough here. What's worried you?"

"I've never found it easy to fit in, and I confess I've had troubles a time or two. Some of the men in the apartments I lived in figured out that I wasn't human. Blamed me for equipment and gadgets nearby breaking. The elevator, people's TVs, things like that," he said.

As he finished speaking, someone else knocked on the door. Daisy and I both moved closer to it, the one-way privacy glass allowing us to see the group of four men on the other side of it. They were muscular, and two of them had arms covered in tattoos. The expression on the one closest made me sigh.

It was clear they were after the dwarf. I glanced at our visitor and then at Daisy. She moved to his side as Zephyr appeared.

I quickly filled Zephyr in on what was happening, using my mental abilities. Then I reached for the door handle again.

"No, don't let them in. They're angry, and there's no

knowing what they'll do." The dwarf backed up, looking as if he might run anywhere he thought was safe.

"We defeated an entire agency with guns and all sorts of other stuff. I'm sure I can handle four men who got the wrong end of the stick."

Without giving the dwarf any more time to panic, I opened the door. The men looked surprised to see me, their eyes going wide as they took in my appearance. I wasn't sure they recognized me, but I decided not to take the chance.

"Hi," I said. "I'm Aella. You guys might have heard of me. I'm the elf. How can I help you? Are you here to join the dojo?"

"You run this dojo?" the ringleader said.

"No. My friend runs it, actually. She got it up and running while I was fleeing for my life one month." I grinned as I spoke, trying to make it clear that I wasn't bothered about it. "Do you want to come in and have a look around?"

They all looked at each other before the first one shrugged. I backed up, allowing them entrance. After hesitating for a moment, they came inside with me.

While we'd been talking, Zephyr had moved, coming to stand in full view. He was the first thing they saw.

I was used to people finding Zephyr intimidating, but with these men it was a whole other level. Their mouths dropped open, and they simply stopped and stared.

"This is Zephyr. Don't worry, he doesn't bite unless you're trying to kill me or one of my friends. And do I understand correctly that you know our dwarven friend here?"

I brought their attention back to the dwarf and Daisy, who were both standing by the reception desk.

The guy looked at him before nodding.

"Great," I continued, not giving anyone a chance to say anything they might regret. "It always makes it a bit easier for humans coming here the first time if they already know a mythical. Let me give you the tour."

I led them up to the changing area and then down through to the warehouse on the other side, telling them here and there about how it had been when we'd first been living in the building. And how nice it was to have the building so busy and so full of life now.

At first they barely said anything, but they looked around and took everything in. It was only as Ronan offered to give them archery lessons and two of them got really excited that it seemed to break the ice.

Sighing with relief, I left the four of them in very capable hands.

"I'll see our new dwarf friend is escorted home and make sure he feels safe," Daisy said as I made my way back toward the stairs.

I couldn't be sure, but I thought there was a new little light in her eyes as she went back to her charge and struck up another conversation. I watched the two of them walk away, grateful.

Come on, Zephyr said. *Time for a break.*

I looked straight to the dragon, still at my side, and smiled. I couldn't think of anything better.

CHAPTER THREE

I groaned as noises from around me woke me up the following morning. Then Zephyr moved, taking his tail away. It had been both my pillow and my blanket, and it gave me no choice but to move.

Wake up, sleepyhead, Zephyr said as he stood and shook.

Why do we have to live with so many other people? I asked him a moment later.

Because they needed a place to stay and this is a warehouse, not an apartment house.

I sighed. He was right.

We needed to do something about it. *Could we build upward?* Daisy had said she would be looking into it. It would solve a lot of our problems.

Immediately I imagined some city council rejecting a planning application because we were mythicals and they didn't want to see us band together.

There was also the matter of how we'd pay for it all and if the foundations could handle it. The dojo was bringing in money, but it also had a lot of dependents and mouths to feed. To add to that, the organization were still being funny about paying me or Erlan anything. It wasn't a source of funds I trusted entirely, but so far, only Chris and Minsheng were getting any money from them.

Minsheng still had his restaurants, but I felt bad asking him to pay for my schemes. I needed to find a way to earn money. And fast. Well, more money. Lyra was paying a small amount for using the warehouse as a dojo from its profits.

As for the foundations, we needed to check based on the old plans for the initial construction, but they were proving elusive.

After dressing and getting ourselves clean, Zephyr and I headed to the kitchen to get some breakfast. We found Daisy there with Chris, poring over some drawings.

"We're going to need a bathroom or two," she said. "And showers. It's bad enough everyone coming in and out of the dojo can't shower."

"You doing what I think you are?" I asked.

"Yeah. Chris found a law that said a building can be modified internally and walls moved without planning permission as long as it doesn't exceed the footprint or height of the tallest point," Daisy replied.

"Which means we can build a more permanent full floor above as long as it's light enough the walls and support can handle it and it doesn't get taller than the exit up there was."

I exhaled with relief and told them I'd been having similar thoughts as I grabbed us both a quick breakfast and we started to munch.

"I know an architect who said he'd spec some of it free, so we're making a list of wants."

"Somewhere big enough for Zephyr longer term," I said immediately.

Finally, someone is thinking of me.

I think of you all the time.

You have me in your head. There's a difference.

I still think of you. It might sometimes be, "grrrrr why can't I have a thought he won't hear," but it's still thinking of you.

I heard Zephyr chuckle and noticed Daisy giving us a look.

"You know it's rude to have secretive conversations that others can't hear while they're around," Daisy said. "If the two of you are going to crack jokes about what we're doing, then you can go do something else."

I looked apologetic before getting up. If Daisy and Chris were handling my accommodation problem and bearing in mind Zephyr's size, then I didn't need to be part of the conversation anymore. With pretty much no money to offer and no architectural skills, I was better off going back to the tasks I did best.

Training, protecting, and fighting.

Ronan's demonstration of archery the evening before had given me an idea.

At the moment, the dojo was only occupying about half the warehouse space. We could partition off some floor space and use it as both a shooting range and an archery range. While there were already plenty of shooting ranges in the country, there were fewer archery ranges, and the demand for them was going up. Not only that, but I liked the idea of learning a new skill.

I found Ronan monitoring the security cameras again, taking his role as our security supervisor very seriously. It had come naturally to him anyway, his previous occupation having been night guard at the Sanctuary.

He'd been the first person we'd met when entering the dome that protected the mythicals living inside.

Of course, it had moved now. Twice.

Ronan had opted to come with us and try to change the world rather than hide from humans for as long as possible.

As soon as he saw me, he smiled.

"Thank you for yesterday," I said. "You made a big difference with those fellas."

"I don't think all of them were convinced we were friendly, but two of them wanted to know if we were going to start archery lessons. They handed me cards with information I didn't understand, but they assured me other humans would."

I laughed and nodded before explaining.

"And about the archery lessons," I said as soon as there was a chance. "Would you teach me?"

"If you'll get someone to teach me how to use a gun," Ronan replied.

I blinked for a moment, surprised by the request. Ronan had always looked right with a bow slung over his back. There was something about the idea of him using a gun that seemed so out of the ordinary. But the more I thought about it, the more I realized it made sense.

Was I just being sentimental and romantic about fantasy stories to think learning how to use a bow would be a good idea? I wasn't sure, but I couldn't spend all my time learning with only one thing in mind. Every now and then, I should get to learn something because I wanted to, or I enjoyed it.

"You've got a deal," I said. "Daisy's our best marksman, but if she's too busy, I can start teaching you what I know."

Zephyr huffed off to one side, clearly not impressed by the idea of me learning yet another thing that didn't really involve him. I knew he meant it good-naturedly, but I'd not had very much success trying to move around the gas he created or control it.

Minsheng had been measuring it and assured me it had gotten more potent as Zephyr had grown, but that had only made me more wary. If I got it wrong, I could knock out other people.

We could train on the roof, Zephyr suggested. *At least, while it is a roof and not apartments.*

Not a bad idea. If you can persuade Minsheng to add it back into our training schedule, we'll do it.

Then have fun with your archery. I'm off to find our Shishou.

For a moment I watched Zephyr walk away. Had I not been taking his annoyance at our lack of joint training seriously? Was I focusing a bit too much on what I could learn and not on what we could achieve together?

I sighed. There were so many people to accommodate now, I was sure I was neglecting some. It was like I was being pulled in a load of different directions at once, and I wasn't sure what was best.

As Ronan moved the archery targets into place, however, I decided to push it from my mind for a moment.

I needed time off now and then too. And I'd already made a deal with Ronan.

The half an hour he taught me to shoot arrows slipped by incredibly quickly. I found the larger projectiles easier to help with my abilities, my mind doing so naturally.

Although my first few shots barely hit the target, my latter ones grew closer to the gold rings in the center. Even when my shot was going wide, I used the air to funnel it toward the goal.

It was practice I was sure Minsheng would have been proud of even if he might not have approved of the bow. And it served to emphasize that I was starting to use my abilities automatically and without thinking. They were becoming a part of me rather than something I had to focus on.

I had no idea if that was healthy or not, but it was continuing to make me stronger and more efficient.

It didn't take long to switch the archery targets for shooting ones and then I was showing Ronan how a gun worked. It was a different grip and mechanism to the bow, but the principle was the same. Point and shoot. I'd seen him with a taser in the past, no doubt taken off one of the agents, but even that was a little different.

His first shot went way too high, embedding in the wall just above the target before I remembered that in archery, you have to aim a little higher to allow for some curve. I chuckled and then explained that you could aim the gun more true.

Before Ronan could take another shot, his eyes seemed to glaze over, like he'd gone into some sort of trance.

Worried he wasn't okay but not wanting to call out in

case it triggered some kind of reaction in Ronan while he held a gun, I looked for someone to get Minsheng.

Thankfully, my Shishou and Zephyr were already coming back.

He's talking to his commander at the Sanctuary, Zephyr said into my head before I could even ask if he knew what was going on. *This is normal for their kind. They'll be sharing visions and memories, possibly even sharing what they can see right now.*

Does that mean the Sanctuary is in danger?

Maybe.

I moved closer to Zephyr and filled Minsheng in on everything Zephyr had just said, keeping my voice down as I did.

"Then I guess we wait for him to return to us," Minsheng whispered. "Hopefully it won't be anything too serious. The only agent who knew where the Sanctuary was is now dead. It's unlikely that they're in danger."

I tried to smile and let Minsheng's words reassure me, but I knew this wasn't likely to be a friendly catch-up over tea and cookies. Whatever someone had contacted Ronan for, it was going to be important. It just remained to be seen if it was the good kind of important or the bad.

Zephyr and Minsheng moved toward the usual training section of the room, clearly ready for us to begin training for the day, but I couldn't bring myself to leave Ronan's side.

Worried about the gun he held, dangling from one arm at his side, I slowly moved to stand beside him and not in front of it and reached to take it from his hands.

For a moment his hand seemed to clutch it a little

tighter, but slowing my approach was enough to make him relax again, as if it had been a reflex to me initiating contact. Over the next minute, I eased the weapon out of his hand, unloaded it and put it away in a locked cabinet.

By the time I was done, Minsheng was clearly trying to get my attention. I ignored him, still sticking close to Ronan. It felt odd to leave him when he wasn't properly in his body. He was vulnerable even if the warehouse was safe.

Minsheng was coming over, no doubt to encourage me to train and leave Ronan when Ronan suddenly moved and blinked. Instantly I was grateful I'd slipped the gun out of his hands. Although Ronan was still facing the targets and not the people, he'd definitely have fired and I was pretty sure it would have been in a fairly random direction.

If the original path hadn't been likely to hurt someone, there was a good chance the bullet would have ricocheted and caught someone on the rebound.

"Forgive me," Ronan said. "Lorcan felt it was important I see something, and I fear he was right."

Although Ronan was regularly serious, his tone now made it clear he was bothered by the news he'd just acquired.

"What's happened?" I asked as Minsheng and Zephyr came closer, both clearly listening.

"The council believes that someone is targeting the orbs that lead to the Sanctuary."

"Targeting them? To try to get to the Sanctuary?"

"Perhaps. But three are missing, and many, many more have been destroyed."

I gasped, instantly thinking of the orb I'd been given

only a few weeks previously. Was this what the threat had meant?

"How do they know?" Minsheng asked a moment later. His tone was soft and non-accusatory, but he clearly wanted more info.

"A new group arrived at the Sanctuary together. Yesterday, I believe. They came as most do, led by an orb. But the group was large, and not everyone knew each other well. An assortment of mixed-race mythicals who had realized their true nature but been ostracized since our revelation to humanity."

"We've been getting the same here," I replied, not sure what that significance had to do with the story Ronan was relating.

"They'd all been looking for orbs for some weeks."

"As a group?"

"No. They had joined forces as each of them had failed to find orbs or come across broken ones."

I frowned. The Sanctuary had made a point of finding out which orb I'd used so they could replace it. There shouldn't have been lots missing.

"Do they know what's happened to them?" I asked, but I suspected they didn't. Otherwise, why would they be telling Ronan?

He shook his head. "They've asked me to go to an orb near a cluster that has gone missing and see if that one is still there. And to replace some if I can. The Sanctuary has spares I could pick up. We may need to hide them in different ways going forward, however. They were never supposed to be easy to find."

"I'll come with you," I said as I went to the box I'd

received. I'd not shown it to anyone else, but I got it out now and showed Ronan. "I have an idea of who might be behind this but no confirmation of it."

Ronan frowned.

"I wish you'd shared this when it happened."

"It was sent to me after a TV appearance, and I thought the threat was meant for me only. It's clear I was wrong. I can only ask for your forgiveness and for the opportunity to help protect the Sanctuary going forward."

Ronan bowed lower.

"That you seek to protect others is reason enough I would allow your assistance and even ask for it. But it is often easier to protect oneself with more of the facts."

"Noted," I replied, putting the lid back on the mangled orb. It wasn't a pretty sight, even if it had turned out to be fake blood on it.

Guess I'd better go pack then, Zephyr said as we started to put the equipment away and Minsheng began making a list of supplies we'd need.

What could you possibly bring? I asked. *And where would you put your luggage?*

If I didn't have to lug you around wherever we went, I could carry a lot. A cuddly toy, food, granola bars. Maybe even a tent or something so I don't get rained on so much.

I shook my head, trying not to laugh out loud. At least I could trust Zephyr to keep me from getting too serious.

CHAPTER FOUR

Eventually we'd settled on a small group to travel. I'd insisted we travel in the armored vehicle Ronan's friend had lent us several months earlier, not least because it was the only vehicle we had left that was big enough for Zephyr. Also because we had Ronan with us and we didn't know what problem we would be facing.

If it had been just Zephyr and I going, I'd not have even bothered with that but flown and carried a tent or something with us to camp somewhere along the way, but Ronan was the only one who knew what we were looking for and the Sanctuary had asked for his aid personally. I couldn't leave him behind or let him fend for himself, especially when the journey might be dangerous.

We traveled for some time, Zephyr and I riding on the top as we had previously. Even now, Zephyr didn't fit that well inside the vehicle. He wouldn't fit at all eventually, and it was yet another reason we were going to have to begin flying everywhere together independently. With us we had Daisy and the dwarf who'd dropped by the dojo.

He'd turned up to say thank you, handing Daisy a bouquet of flowers that hadn't gone unnoticed, and then, when he saw her packed bag and she had mentioned the Sanctuary, Holfin pretty much demanded we take him there.

It was a place most mythicals had heard of. Apparently Holfin had always wanted to find it, and he'd tried to find some orbs in the past.

At first I'd objected, not wanting to endanger another mythical who might not understand the perils of our journey. Daisy had been all for it, however.

She'd made a good point about it being the guy's choice and said the life of a mythical had been dangerous for a long time. No one was in any more danger than they had been before I made our existence public.

With that, we'd had our group.

It felt strange to be traveling without Minsheng or Erlan and Newton, but they'd opted to stay behind to keep training and continue pushing Daisy's plans to expand the warehouse.

Given Erlan was also trying to get into Crawley's laptop for me, I considered it the best use of all of our time. This was just something I was going to have to get used to.

We traveled along to Arizona and then a little North. I'd brought my orb with me, so I was pretty sure we had been going in the direction of the Sanctuary at first, but we were going more parallel to the route I thought we should be taking now.

I sighed as the miles of dusty road went by. We'd been up in the Rockies but were coming down the other side again now. We'd both slept a little through the night, but thanks to Holfin being able to drive the bus, we hadn't stopped.

I sighed as I thought about all the traveling we'd been doing back and forth. The last time I'd headed to the Sanctuary, I'd been excited and a little apprehensive, but this time I wasn't so sure.

There were some familiar faces I'd be pleased to see, but they'd not been happy about how much danger I'd put them in the first time. If it was Jacobs taking the orbs, I couldn't imagine they'd be happy this time either.

We weren't much further down the road when we took a right, bumping down a dirt track that couldn't have been on the map.

There were a few trees here and there, but nothing significant. Zephyr flew up into the air the third time the vehicle hit a pothole and lurched, and I joined him a couple of seconds later.

I didn't know if the reduced weight made it easier on the others, but it certainly felt more comfortable to fly after all the jolting. Quickly, Zephyr and I came together in the air and I settled onto his back, finding my usual more comfortable spot to ride while he flew.

He lifted up high enough we could see for miles and then followed the car along the dusty track. Even with the camouflaged coloring, it was easy to follow the dust cloud it kicked up.

We passed a few large ranch farms, but no one seemed to pay us much attention, and then the area slowly grew more lush, trees growing with more strength and the ground changing color. We hadn't gone much farther when I spotted a lake up ahead. The dirt track led up to the trees on this edge and then disappeared into a wooded area.

Wherever it went underneath the tree canopy, if it continued anywhere, we couldn't see.

Without needing any prompting from me, Zephyr swooped down and landed by the side of the road just before the trees. The vehicle came up only a minute or so later, slowing and stopping just under the shade of the trees on this edge. It didn't look like the road kept going.

Before I could go inside the forest, everyone got out, Daisy carrying her backpack and a drink bottle she handed me. I took it gratefully and let Ronan lead us toward the lake. It was colder in the shade of the trees, although it was also more still.

Zephyr struggled to come with us, the trees close enough together in some places that he had to squeeze between them.

You okay? I asked when he'd had to pretty much knock another tree over to get through.

If we could have just landed on the edge of the lake instead, I might be.

I frowned as I started to see water ahead, but before we could reach it and the thinner area of the trees, Ronan stopped and looked around. He then made an almost ninety-degree turn and headed right.

We followed until the trees opened up and a stream ran out of the lake. Sitting in one particular place in this stream, dividing it and making the water run either side, was the stump of a tree that looked like it had once been hit by lightning.

Ronan waded through the water and cleared away a

section of broken branches until he unearthed a box similar to the one we'd found our orb in. He opened it to reveal another perfectly intact orb.

"That's something, at least," he said, running a hand over it to activate it.

The light came on and moved to one edge of the orb, making me realize how dark it was getting under the trees. It must have been later than I'd expected.

I pulled my own orb out and checked they were both aiming for the same place. They were, and this seemed to satisfy Ronan.

With a flick of his hand I didn't entirely follow, he deactivated the orb again and started to put it back.

As he was covering it up again, Zephyr suddenly turned, growling. I reached for him.

What is it?

I heard something. We're not alone.

"Company," I whispered just loudly enough that everyone else would hear me.

Speeding up, Ronan continued to hide the orb and then fetch his bow off his back while Daisy pulled out one of the tranquilizer guns she'd taken off an agent at some point.

Lead the way, Zephyr. If someone is here to tamper with the orbs, we need to stop them.

You should guard it.

I'd rather catch them. I can move faster than anyone else.

Which one of your friends do you want to ask to keep it safe then?

None of you, but that doesn't mean I'm the best person for the job. It just means I care too much. Plus, you're not supposed to split the party, ever. Everyone who plays games knows that.

Last I checked, this wasn't a game.

Zephyr and I fell silent, the witty comeback lost in the distraction of another sound. A bush rustled up ahead, and a figure ran.

Increasing my speed, I ran after them and tried catch them, but they either knew this wood better, or I got confused in the dark because I lost them and had to stop.

Panting, I waited for Zephyr and the others to catch up, but only Zephyr appeared at my side.

What was that about not splitting the party? he asked.

Shitsticks, I replied. *Where are the others?*

Ronan is guarding the orb. Daisy is taking Holfin back to the armored vehicle, where it's safest.

Immediately, I was torn. I knew the orb was important, and I didn't want the centaur to be alone, but equally Daisy and Holfin were the most in need of my aid. Ronan had guarded the Sanctuary alone night after night for decades. He knew what he was doing.

I'll go back to the vehicle too. Go help Ronan. Zephyr looked at me as he finished speaking into my head. I nodded. It wasn't a perfect solution, but it was a solution.

I didn't like the idea of being away from Zephyr, but I didn't trust anyone more than him to stay safe. He was bulletproof and so strong most people didn't stand a chance against him. And if he was with Daisy and Holfin, they'd be a lot safer.

But that meant I needed to try to get back to Ronan. With the forest getting darker and darker, could I find him?

Just follow Ronan's logic. Put the water on your left and keep walking till you get to the stream. Then walk away from the lake.

Good point. Glad someone was paying attention.

Glad I was paying attention you mean, Zephyr replied as we walked away from each other.

Something like that. I felt him get further away, the strange feeling of something unraveling deep inside me. It almost made me turn back and go after him, but I had to trust he'd be fine. We'd been training for things like this.

Slowly, while listening and looking for signs of others around me, I made my way back in the direction I thought Ronan was.

I was beginning to think I must have gone too far or wrong somewhere, the forest beginning to look the same in every direction, but I could just see the setting sun glinting off the lake to my left still.

Telling myself I'd just keep going for a few more minutes, I reached for Zephyr with my mind.

Are the others safe? I asked, hoping he'd hear.

We're all back at the truck. No sign of trouble.

Zephyr's voice sounded quieter than normal in my head, but it was phenomenal that he could hear me at all. We'd once been separated over a large distance on a beach when we'd been trying to hide from people, and I'd lost contact with him. The distance then had been less than it was now. Our bond was clearly growing.

There was a splash as I stuck my foot in the small stream before I'd even realized it was there. Sighing, I turned away from the lake and followed the winding babbling water. It was noisy enough I'd struggle to hear noises from anyone sneaking around, but it also meant I was going in the right direction.

As I kept walking, I started to imagine all sorts of other

scenarios. What if Ronan wasn't there? Would I have to somehow find my way back to the vehicle alone? And probably in the dark?

You could just come to me, Zephyr reminded me, making it clear he was still listening out for me. And it was a good point. I instantly felt better. While he was close enough to feel mentally, I could also tell roughly what direction.

I sped up, sure that Ronan might need me if Zephyr and the others were still not in danger. Odds were that whoever had been here was going to head back to the orb.

As I went around the next bend I noticed the tree that split the stream but there was no sign of Ronan. Until I got closer, and Ronan moved an arm, bringing his finger to his lips.

He was standing a little way from the orb, the rest of his body perfectly still and hiding in the shadows of a large tree.

Carefully, I picked my way over to another large tree not far from him and turned to focus on the orb as he had. It hadn't even occurred to me that instead of standing out in the open, protecting the orb, he'd be watching it and keeping it safe from elsewhere.

It made sense, given Ronan's style and the way he'd guarded the Sanctuary, but I was so used to combat being confrontational and standing my ground, I hadn't thought through the best way to protect something like this and find out who had come for it at the same time.

More time ticked by, and the forest grew even darker. I considered giving up several times, not sure this was worth it, but I knew Ronan didn't want to give up, and the Sanctuary meant a lot more to him than it did to me.

If he was happy to stay and keep an eye out, then so was I.

A noise drew my attention more than once, but it was always some wildlife, a bird in the bushes or a rustling rabbit or mouse. Never anything larger and more sinister. More than once I saw a deer, but we kept ourselves still enough it didn't appear to notice us and continued on its travels.

The next time I heard movement I was ready to assume it was another bird, but a glint caught my eye, and someone thin with a feminine frame and dark clothing appeared by the edge of the stream.

She only had eyes for the tree protecting the orb and went straight toward it.

I shifted behind the large tree in front of me, trying to get a better look at the woman, but it wasn't clear who she was. She had either painted her face with something dark or was wearing a thin mask, her skin almost entirely covered. There was a ponytail just about showing when she turned her head, also startled by a bird for a moment.

The animal almost got shot, the woman pulling her gun. She held it in a very natural grip and had reached for it almost instinctively, so whoever this was, they'd had at least a little weapons training.

As she stepped into the stream, Ronan made his move, unslinging his bow and aiming an arrow at her.

"Stop right there," he called, but instead of listening, she fired her gun in his direction. I tried to use my powers to blast the bullet and the gun, but I only caught the weapon, sending it off to the side and out of her grip.

As she fled I rushed after her, and Ronan fired. The

arrow flew in her direction, but both of them had disappeared past a bush and I couldn't see if it hit. I thought I heard a grunt of pain, but I was too concerned about Ronan.

The centaur was leaning against the tree nearby, a hand pressed to his shoulder.

"You're shot?" I half-asked and half-declared, staying put when I knew I should have probably gone after the woman.

"Yes, but it only clipped me. I'll live. I hit her too. We should pursue her."

I frowned, intending to argue, but Ronan didn't give me any choice and ran into the woods in the direction she'd gone.

Using my abilities to speed my passage, I ran after.

Here and there, Ronan paused, pointing out scuff marks or blood splatters to let us know we were still on the right trail. There was little I could do but keep Zephyr informed and follow, however.

We were quickly heading back toward the vehicle and Zephyr, my awareness of him getting stronger again. I tried not to panic as it became clear that whoever this woman was, she was heading in their direction.

Make sure Daisy and Holfin are inside, I told Zephyr, grateful that he was bulletproof. I then hurried to catch up with Ronan despite beginning to feel both physical fatigue and mental from using my abilities to propel myself along so much.

Before we reached Zephyr and the others, however, we came across a small clearing. The blood spots went up to a single place where there was a cluster of drops and a bloody object. Ronan rushed over and picked up one end of his arrow.

I rushed toward the edge of the clearing where a dirt track led away from the lake in time to see the woman riding away on a motorcycle. She was already far away.

Briefly I considered flying after her and getting Zephyr to meet me partway, but Ronan was panting hard behind me, and another look at the wound on his shoulder convinced me he needed me more. It had only grazed him, but the wound was still pretty deep, and it was bleeding more than I liked to see.

"Come on," I said. "We've protected the orb. Let's get you patched up."

Ronan nodded, his large eyes looking more than a little tired. I hurried to his side and let him lean on me as we made our way toward the others.

CHAPTER FIVE

Sitting and leaning against Zephyr, we bounced along as the large vehicle beneath us continued to eat up the miles. Ronan was resting in the back, his wounds seen to by Daisy. She'd even stitched him up, showing once again that she had a thorough understanding of how to help the wounded. With her ability to fire a gun, I was starting to suspect Daisy had served somewhere. She'd told me she's trained to shoot because she'd wanted to be useful like her brother when he became a Shishou, but was that the full story?

Now Daisy had rested for a bit, Holfin was also asleep. It was the early hours of the morning and I'd dozed here and there, but I couldn't get my mind to rest, not helped by the bumpy road we traveled on.

We'd been traveling down an older route for some time, the Sanctuary getting close enough that the major roads were all going to lead us away rather than closer, but we still weren't there.

We'd had to travel through a few small towns, but few

were up to even notice Zephyr and me sitting on top of the vehicle. Those who did either waved or stared, and Zephyr had gotten pretty good at wiggling one of his front claws in something akin to a wave.

Now, however, we were out in the middle of nowhere, and it was eerily quiet.

I can't get past the idea that I knew that woman, I said to Zephyr as I thought back to the incident.

She was probably an agent.

Probably.

But that didn't bode well, because if she was an agent I was familiar with, that meant that either Crawley was still operating or Jacobs had kept the branch serving him despite Crawley no longer being involved.

What if it was Crawley? I asked a moment later.

What if it was? She is still an agent. We don't know for sure that she just ran and didn't look back. She might be as angry with you as Jacobs. She might have sent that note and the orb we received.

I suppose it might be her and not Jacobs behind the whole thing with the other orbs and the Sanctuary's problems.

That too.

I sighed. Was I really never going to be free of the agency and the fear and misunderstanding they represented?

Some people don't find it easy to change. It's not a process people like to accept or acknowledge. Most people don't even seem to be able to grow.

You can't grow when you're blaming others for your problems all the time, I replied.

True. Which is why we need to make sure we're keeping ourselves in check.

What do you mean?

Ronan shot that woman today.

She shot him first.

Yes, but Chris also killed Knox. Do we want to be people who kill? We're stronger than almost everyone around us. In most fights we don't need to kill. Most people coming up against us are just following orders.

True. I can't dictate that the others risk their lives more because we don't want to kill though.

Can you truly not? I think they'd understand.

I let out another loud exhale, more than a little frustrated. When had Zephyr become the mature one? He was right, of course. We needed to find a way to defend ourselves without killing others or even hurting them if possible, like we had in the past.

I'd demonstrated my unwillingness to harm if I didn't have to by always lowering agents down from heights I'd blown them off, always using tranquilizer guns instead of ones with bullets, and knocking people out temporarily with Zephyr's gas over killing them.

But was it always going to be possible to knock people out rather than kill them? I had no idea. I'd hoped this battle was going to be over, but it was beginning to feel like every victory led to something bigger and worse, and along the way, I gained more people who were depending on me for protection.

Always the way for the strong. People who need that strength gravitate toward it. But now and then, some come along who want to help too. We've got good support. Tuviel and Azargad never had so many strong friends around them, and they managed to unite a broken world and protect it from all sorts of dangers.

I sighed, grateful that Zephyr could now remember so much of his ancestors' pasts. He always seemed to know what to say.

Before I could worry any more about our future, the orb light started to move more obviously, an indicator that we were close. I knew Daisy had another orb in the front of the vehicle with her, but I still gave the roof a double tap on the side of the cab so she'd know I was giving instructions to take the next right.

We ended up heading down a dirt track, and then the orb seemed to point steadily dead ahead of us.

Once more I felt the growing compulsion to head toward something. To go on an adventure of sorts. Then, as we rounded a corner, I saw it. Another—different, but still majestic—elven city rose up before us.

This one sat in the trees in the dry sand surroundings, the city the only place with lush vegetation and bright colors.

I was slightly surprised that I could see it. Given the place had moved, I'd half-expected it to be closed off again. Instead, it was right there for me to find. It made me wonder if anyone else could always find it or if Knox would have been able to. Maybe it was for the best that Chris had killed him.

We didn't get much closer before Daisy pulled over, a small lookout hut having appeared in one of the trees.

No sooner had we pulled over than a gnome I'd not met the last time I was in the Sanctuary scurried down, practically sliding down the ladder in an attempt to reach us faster.

"Well met," I said from on top, Zephyr at my side and already getting to his feet to get down. "We've been to the Sanctuary in a previous location and I have Ronan with me. We have news for the council."

The gnome looked like he might reply with something negative until Ronan opened the back hatch and climbed out, his injury obvious.

"Aella speaks the truth. We have news and a mission they gave me to personally report on."

"Of course, Ronan. If these folks are all with you, then I can see no harm. Please continue. But I would urge caution. The name 'Aella' is not spoken of entirely with admiration within the Sanctuary. Things have changed in the world, and fear of new threats makes some wary."

"Understood, Grelbeck," Ronan replied as he got back inside, clearly hurting still.

I frowned and sat back down, not sure how I felt about the gnome's warning. I appreciated it, but I had been hoping for a warmer reception.

As Grelbeck said, change is often feared, Zephyr projected into my head. *And we've changed everything.*

Let us hope it is for the better.

In time it will be, but for now...who knows.

You're not making me feel any better.

If you wanted someone to make you feel better about yourself you should probably have bonded with a mermaid. Or a cheerleader.

I rolled my eyes. I wasn't sure I had a choice.

We all know even if you had, you'd have chosen me anyway. I'm the great majestic and powerful dragon.

Are you sure we're widening the doorways for your body? I'm beginning to think your head's what we need more room for.

Zephyr let out a humph, but his mouth slipped open into the usual teeth-filled grin.

I leaned into him, grateful for my one constant.

After traveling for about half a mile more, we reached the edge of the city and everyone piled out. There wasn't anywhere specifically to park, so Daisy just stuck it out of the way and we walked between the different houses. Although this version of the city wasn't built on a lake, it did appear to harmonize with nature in a similar way.

Again I marveled at the beauty, but it was the middle of the night, so I couldn't see very far. Only the lit-up areas.

We were near the council building when someone came running out to us.

"The council has asked to know if your matter is urgent or if it could wait until morning," the new gnome asked Ronan.

"It can wait," Ronan replied. "But if so, we will need beds for two dwarves, an elf, an almost fully grown dragon, and myself."

I lifted my eyebrows at the list, having rarely heard myself referred to as an elf and thinking Ronan had made a mistake for a moment. But I was at least part-elf, and according to Zephyr, looking more elven as time went by. I tried not to think about it too much and instead followed on as we were led away.

There was only one suitable guest house, a large open-plan building with arches into the main living area and small flower-like pods that doubled as soft beds.

"This was meant for a family of dryads and wood nymphs, but if you all feel comfortable here, it is the best building to accommodate a dragon."

Behind me I heard Zephyr sigh, but Daisy was so excited that she ran up to the first pod and climbed straight into the center of the open flower. I grinned and nodded at the gnome.

Even Ronan managed to settle himself into one of the larger ones.

"Well, this is one of the strangest things I've ever done, but if it's comfortable, I'm game to try it," Holfin said before picking another.

As the gnome scurried away and Zephyr settled into the middle of the floor, I went over to him.

You don't want to sleep in a flower? he asked.

Not unless there's one big enough for both of us, I replied.

The following morning dawned bright, and birdsong woke me. Zephyr was still warm beside me and snoring softly. I considered wriggling out from underneath the tail that was half-draped over me, but it was warm, and I ached from the pursuit and hard work of the day before. While I had fairly good fitness, it clearly wasn't that good.

I'd only been awake for a couple of minutes when the gnome reappeared.

As I was the only one awake, I got to my feet to meet

him. At first he appeared startled to see me emerge from beside the dragon, but then he nodded.

"The council will see you as soon as you're able," he said.

"We'll be there in a few minutes," I replied, feeling Zephyr come awake in my mind rather than see it.

This seemed to make the others stir as well. The flower petals that had curled up around their occupants opened and allowed them to alight. In each case, when the person inside was ready, a petal would bend entirely down on one side so they could slide down it and land on their feet.

The most impressive was seeing Ronan do this. He slid sideways and landed upright, his bow on his back and his injured shoulder looking much better. He'd removed the dressing Daisy had put on it, and it had begun healing. Once more, I was grateful that all mythicals seemed to heal faster than humans.

"Given the council asked me to investigate on their behalf, it is probably best if I do most of the talking," Ronan said as he looked at me. "But I understand if you wish to take the task."

"No," I replied, shaking my head. "I do not need to feel like I am in charge of something merely for the sake of it, nor to appear it for my own ego. You understand the council and what they need and want far better than me, and this was, as you've said, your investigation. Please, lead the way. I'm merely here to help."

Ronan bowed and trotted out of the building into the sunlight.

Thankfully we weren't far from the council, but the walk over was awkward more than once. Those inhabitants of the city who were already up and moving about seemed intent on staring or whispering, and it was clear I was the subject, their eyes frequently on me.

I tried not to worry about it, thinking more of the task I was there for. Finding out what had happened to the orbs and how we could protect more of them.

While I hoped something like the Sanctuary would soon no longer be necessary, we were still far from that point in life, and until then, it was a harbor for many who needed a safe haven, or simply wanted to learn of their own kind after many years in the dark.

The council was all gathered in a building very similar to the one at the last city, a central staircase leading up into a room suspended inside a tree. Zephyr flew up the outside this time, and I made a point of going with him, using my abilities to bring me up the sides and drop in through the top.

Ronan stepped up onto the landing as Zephyr and I landed. Despite his being our leader on this, all eyes went to me, and for a moment, I wondered if I should have taken the stairs.

Instead, I stepped back, not daring to look at anyone as I purposefully and obviously gave way to Ronan. The council sat but didn't offer us the same courtesy.

"As you are probably aware by now, council, we are here to report on the investigation Lorcan tasked me with and the protection of another Sanctuary orb nearby," Ronan said to begin.

"I can see that, but I wasn't expecting quite such a large entourage," Sierrathen said, looking at Daisy and the dwarf by her side.

Ronan bowed and explained who everyone was, making sure my name was mentioned as well. When there was little response except to offer Holfin a home if he wished for one, I tried not to fume. It was clear the invitation was for him alone, and Daisy, Zephyr, and I were far less welcome to stick around.

Ignoring it for now, Ronan told our story, making sure they were aware that the orb was safe, but someone had known of it and would likely return to finish the job. It didn't take long since Ronan kept the story concise.

"Had Aella not risked her life in coming out to the orb with me, I suspect the woman would have obtained the orb anyway and I would have lost my life. I am not used to fighting guns. None of us are. But Aella is, and she knows the dangers the humans of the world can pose far better than I."

I blinked, surprised by his final words. Ronan had just essentially told the council he supported me and my actions and stressed that I had been there for him when they hadn't. I could only bow to him and hope he understood how grateful I was.

CHAPTER SIX

The council sat in silence for almost a full minute following Ronan's closing statement, and it almost grew awkward. At least, more awkward than it had felt at the beginning.

"It is clear that the Sanctuary and the orbs we have placed to guide people here are no longer as safe as we once were. More humans are aware of us than we'd believed, and they clearly mean us harm. Thank you, Ronan, for your service to us once again," Lorcan said. "As always, you are free to go or stay as you please, but we would be honored if you would consider continuing to aiding us should we need it in the future."

"As I always will," he replied.

"We will have the orb moved and rehidden somewhere safer as we've done with many of the others. It can be a matter for later, however."

Again the councilors seemed to purposely ignore me. At least until Lorcan looked straight at me.

"I am also grateful that you acted to save Ronan's life, Aella.

It is a great sacrifice to put oneself in harm's way for another, and it is clear you have earned Ronan's respect both before this and for this. While I won't pretend to understand everything you have done and what it means for our kind, I will ask you to continue to protect him while he is by your side."

"As I endeavor to do for all mythicals no matter where they are," I replied, knowing my tone was loaded but unable to help it.

"Yet you exposed all our kind to humanity."

"I did, yes, because it was the only way to stop an agency with a mandate to keep us secret and make us disappear. The human race isn't fond of financially funding something they know nothing about. Now they know, and many are disgusted. The agency is no more."

"But the humans continue to attack our orbs and look for the Sanctuary."

"Not all humans, but someone, possibly an agent of the agency I am trying to shut down. Rest assured, I am using all my resources to locate this someone. I believe I know who they are, and if I'm right, they are operating in the shadows. A rogue human, as it were. As I have already said. I endeavor to protect all mythicals wherever they are, just as my ancestors did."

"Of course, the great Tuviel. She united us all once, and she had powers beyond anything we've seen since. But I should remind you that you're not her, and you don't have the support she did either."

"No. I don't have the support she finished with, no. But given what I know of people and mythicals, I don't doubt she didn't have full support at the beginning or at the end either. There's something about studying history and then living something new. So many people support someone after they're victorious. It takes bravery to support someone still fighting and struggling to win."

"So you admit you're not sure you can win?"

I sighed and rolled my eyes.

Keep calm, Aella, Zephyr said in my head. *They want nothing more than to bait you.*

Tell me about it, I replied, as I looked at them. Lorcan was the only one who seemed even remotely friendly.

"I'm not sure I can win," I replied, my voice calm once more. "But I don't know anyone who truly ever is. I do know what I've already shown. That I've accepted what I believe to be my role, to protect mythicals, and I will do it to the best of my ability. Help me if you choose. Or don't. That's up to you. I'll do my best anyway."

There was silence as I finished speaking, but I almost thought Sierrathen was going to say something.

"If you have no questions for me or those with me, then I should go. I am needed back in LA and have someone to hunt down. Should you need my assistance, you know where and how to find us." I turned to Zephyr to make it clear I wanted to leave, but before I could the council, all stood up.

"We will discuss what we've heard and what we believe would be appropriate to do next, given this information. We hope that you would continue to share with us any further information pertaining to our safety. In the meantime, we must act how we see fit for the safety of those under our care."

"Of course," I replied. "I look forward to working together to ensure the safety of all mythicals in the future."

It was a political-sounding crap response and I knew it, but it was all I could say. Thankfully Ronan was the first to actually walk away, and it gave me a moment to gather my thoughts and my control of the air before powering upward.

Zephyr caught me in the air and took us even higher.

You handled that well, he said a moment later. *And I can confirm there were many times Tuviel didn't have full support until everyone was defeated and she was victorious or everyone was sure of her victory. Even with a dragon.*

I smirked at the last part, but I was grateful for his words. I'd been bluffing slightly, not knowing if it was true or not but certain I didn't agree with their stance. They were acting out of fear, as others had said. And I didn't have time for it.

As Zephyr landed and the others came close to decide what to do next, I tried to put my anger aside. There was still much I could learn from some of the people here.

"After all that, I'm pretty eager to get back to LA," Daisy said. "I thought they'd be a bit more pleased to see us. Definitely thought they'd show some gratitude for dealing with Knox and protecting their orb."

"While they could have been more respectful, they believe one threat has been swapped for another. I cannot entirely blame their frosty reception, but I too am eager to return to LA. I believe I can defend them more by helping you. We need to find this man and stop him." Ronan's words made me feel instantly calmer.

Daisy looked at Holfin next, looking as if she was about to say goodbye.

"Oh, don't start saying anything so final," Holfin said. "I may have been offered a place to stay, but I think I'm better off with you all in LA. At least, if you'll accept my help. I've been hiding in my apartment most of my life. I'd like to do something more useful. It's clear the people here, or at least the council speaking for them, wish to continue hiding."

Daisy beamed and hugged him.

I stifled a chuckle and nodded.

"I'm pretty sure you're more than welcome to stay with us." I grinned at Daisy as her cheeks flushed red and she let him go.

As one, we made our way back toward the vehicle. I felt like we'd done our good deed for the day, but I couldn't help but feel this trip had been almost entirely wasted.

"You go on ahead. Zephyr and I will catch you up," I said as I spotted what looked like the edge of a training square. Maybe I could learn something new, or at least thank the teachers I'd had the last time I was here.

Zephyr and I went alone toward the square, finding I was right, and the usual elven masters were standing in the four corners with their stalls and gathering students. I'd timed my appearance perfectly to get to learn something.

The water master, Ruehnar, noticed me first, smiling and waving.

"I didn't expect to see your face again for some time," he said, but he seemed to mean it warmly. "Or enjoy the presence of such a fine creature."

As he looked at Zephyr, the dragon lifted his head a little higher and gave his best smile back.

"How has your training been going? Did your attempts to test your water abilities lead anywhere?" he asked, getting straight to one of the reasons I was there.

"I don't think so. I confess that I've tried it only a handful of times, but I think, if there was supposed to be some great point to me being a child of every mastery lineage, then it has failed."

He looked thoughtful for a moment, rubbing his chin with his hand.

"Can you remember the first time you used your air powers?" he asked.

I opened my mouth to reply that it was in Minsheng's training room and that it had come naturally, but I remembered Minsheng asking me if I'd ever run faster or knocked someone or something over. I'd considered it but not truly believed it. Had I used my powers before then?

Thinking back even further, I remembered how agents had seemed to stumble out of my way or fall much harder, and how my previous sensei had often goaded me into anger because he said it made my attacks both faster and stronger.

"I believe I first used them in a fight," I replied eventually. "To defend myself when I was emotional and felt threatened."

"Then perhaps that is what you need. A situation where your ability is needed, and you have very little other way out."

"That sounds dangerous."

The water master chuckled and nodded.

"For some people, life is simply more dangerous than for others. You might not have looked for it, Aella, but yours is to fight for others. And I don't know how or why, but I believe there is more to you than we've seen yet. Keep trying. You may surprise yourself. And even if I'm wrong, at least you will have tried."

I nodded. They were wise words even if it wasn't the answer or information I'd walked into the square for.

Before I could go much further, however, another familiar face came up close. Seth.

The second he entered the square and saw me, he came walking up, clenching his fists, anger clearly his first reaction.

"How dare you," he called loud enough that most of the square went silent and stared our way. "How dare you make our existence public? We've hidden safely for years, and you've endangered us all so you can have ten minutes of fame and power."

I frowned but didn't answer as Zephyr came closer to my side and drew himself up over me. I felt easier knowing he was there to protect me, but I didn't want this to turn into a fight.

"I'll tell you what I've told everyone else. I did what I thought I needed to and what I thought was best. Not everyone agrees with that, but I *know* I've saved lives."

He came up even closer, a couple of inches taller and more muscular as he tried to intimidate me. I didn't back down but I didn't escalate either, merely bringing my air control in tight around me to protect me.

"You're scum, and you're not fit to be wearing Tuviel's necklace, nor to be bonded with a dragon. If you cared about any of us, you'd renounce your bond and let someone else bond with him. Someone who could actually use him to protect everyone."

"Enough, Seth," his elven master said, coming up and putting a hand on his shoulder. "Whether Aella's actions were wrong or right, there is nothing that can be gained from this. She is Tuviel's heir. The necklace would not be around her neck if she were not worthy in Tuviel's eyes. Tuviel herself made sure of that."

"Then maybe Tuviel could make mistakes too."

"I'm sure she could," I replied. "As can all of us. But Zephyr and I are a team, and we're here to learn just like you, so if you'll excuse me, we've got a lesson to get to and a master to listen to."

Before Seth could reply, I walked around him and toward the air master. Thankfully, with his own master there, he didn't follow and allowed me to go to my lesson.

The air master had clearly intended to come and speak to me about something because he smiled as I came closer and ushered me toward his class.

"It is good to see you again, Aella. And my, how much Zephyr has grown. I had always hoped to see a great dragon in the flesh, but I hadn't expected Zephyr to be so much larger already. And still at least six months of growing to do!"

"We're under the understanding that his growth will slow, but already we're encountering problems with living in the human world. Nowhere was designed for a dragon so large."

"I can imagine not. Even here. But you're always welcome, and I shall see what I can do about making sure there's somewhere for you both to sleep in future."

"You can do that?" I asked, aware that people were now listening in around us.

"All should be welcome here, but especially those who wish to aid us. The council will understand the request and the merits of it. They care deeply for all mythicals as well, but they have many duties. You have grown up in the human world, I understand?"

I nodded, not entirely sure where the air master was going but detecting a hint of him being careful what he said and how.

"You have the ability to understand many points of view, that is clear. But come, I was planning on teaching my students how to control and move the air in ways I believe you already have experience. I have been informed that you've had some success creating tornadoes since you were last here?"

A grin spread across my face as I nodded.

Within seconds I was integrated into the lesson again, familiar faces coming up to say hello and one or two even hugging me. It was the warmest welcome Zephyr and I had received since being in the city again, and it made me feel like at least not everyone hated me for what I'd done. It also helped reassure me that for the majority of mythicals in the Sanctuary, life was continuing on as normal.

It was clear, however, after only a few minutes of my lessons, that most of my fellow students were little better than they had been the last time I was there, and I had grown a good deal stronger since.

While we were taking a break and Zephyr was up to something with the other bonded creatures, I made my way toward the air master.

"Is my progress normal?" I asked, deciding to get to the point. "I mean, am I practicing more or finding it easier to grow?"

I trailed off, feeling like I sounded arrogant without meaning to be. I was much more on my guard than I'd ever been.

"You're progressing perfectly and shouldn't be comparing yourself to others. It's clear that you're dedicated. Very few of my students listen so well or clearly practice so much in their own time, but equally, for many of them, it is almost a hobby. They have no pressure to grow, so they dabble and live easier lives."

"Right," I replied, not sure that answered my question but grateful for his wise words nonetheless.

"If you're doubting your abilities long-term or wondering if you are good because you were born that way, then please don't worry. You are indeed blessed with your lineage, and no doubt it makes some elements of your life easier. You have innate talent, but your lineage also brings you many burdens and many other problems. You are neither luckier nor unluckier than the other elves here, just different."

"You sound like the perfect teacher. Someone who sees us all as equals."

"Ah, that is not quite what I mean either. You all have equal potential, but all of you must choose to use your strengths and work to mitigate your weaknesses. Those who work both harder and smarter will achieve far more."

"And is there not luck in that too?"

"Sometimes, of a sort. I am no seer, however, and neither is anyone else. We can only make each decision as it presents itself. But all of us can become the greatest versions of ourselves or not."

Before either of us could say anything else, someone else came up, and Zephyr gave me a nod. It was time for us to leave.

CHAPTER SEVEN

As the armored vehicle rolled through the more densely populated areas of LA and more people noticed us, I started to wonder if Zephyr and I should have gotten in the back and just dealt with how cramped it felt with such a big dragon.

People were staring, and it made it hard to feel even close to relaxed. On top of that, things were tense between Zephyr and me. We'd stayed at the Sanctuary for so long we'd both exhausted ourselves catching up with the others in the vehicle and argued more than once about whether we were going the right way.

It turned out that I was hopeless at directions. The worst part was when I'd agreed to give Zephyr a break from carrying me and flying and then gone in the wrong direction, not realizing he wasn't following.

It had then been hard for Zephyr and me to come back together before we'd found Daisy and Holfin. I was pretty sure Zephyr was still exhausted.

I'm sorry, I said, hoping he'd be listening.

I know. Me too. I just feel like the second-rate sidekick a lot lately. We used to do everything together. Fight the bad guys together.

They like to hide in buildings you can't fit into anymore.

Humans suck.

They can be pretty sensible, though. I mean, they're going to take one look at the big scary dragon and run somewhere only the feeble-looking girl who controls the breeze can get them.

Surely that makes them dumb. They're underestimating you.

People have been underestimating me every moment since we met. So far, it's helped us stay alive, I pointed out.

Good point. Does it bother you?

Sometimes. But it aids us long-term. Would be better if we worked as a team more, though, you're right.

Flying together while you control the air is helping.

True, but I still want to see if we can do cool stuff with your breath.

The air master yesterday. Wasn't he talking about taking control of individual particles?

Yes, I replied, a light bulb coming on in my head. Could I do that with Zephyr's paralyzing gas?

I heard Zephyr chuckle as he waved at a kid on a bicycle. The boy almost swerved into a nearby lamppost but managed to right himself in time.

You've had that thought before now, haven't you?

I wondered when you were first starting to practice tornadoes, but we needed you to make that work then.

Noted. Want to practice gassing people later?

Thought you'd never ask.

The black atmosphere between us disappeared, and both of us waved at anyone looking our way. At least we had a chance of doing good PR while we were traveling.

By the time we were back at the warehouse, my arm was tired, and I had aching cheeks from smiling so much. Minsheng was pleased to see us. I sat with Zephyr in the dining area and ate a huge portion of chow mein while Daisy filled Minsheng in on everything that had happened since we'd left.

Ronan was still injured, but he was regaining some use of the arm and no longer needed the sling. It would be another few days before he could properly pull his bow again, however.

In the meantime, I'd promised to keep teaching him how to use a gun, but it was going to have to wait. As I went to drop my stuff in my room and get what I needed to train with Zephyr for a bit, Erlan popped his head out of a curtained-off area. Newton sat on his shoulder and made a couple of happy little noises when he spotted us.

"Oh, you're back. Here," he said, holding out a familiar laptop. I've reset the password, and you can get into it now."

"You serious?" I asked, blinking. I'd tried to hack into the thing so many times, and he'd done it in the four days I'd been gone.

"Yeah. I'm loving this computer stuff. Minsheng and Chris taught me a bunch, and then I went and found something they call the dark web. Loads of helpful stuff in there. Got it cracked in no time after that."

"You've been on the dark web?"

"Yeah. Chris said I had to be really, really careful, but it's more of a don't connect any computer or laptop that has any kind of secret on it, and, well, mine's brand new and has not been used for literally anything else, so..."

Again I blinked, not sure how to respond. This was genius of a level I didn't understand.

Flicking open the laptop, I immediately settled down with it. Erlan told me the password and showed me what he'd found on there, coming to sit on one side of me. Newton jumped onto his lap and looked at the screen as if he could also read what was up there. Given that Zephyr was sentient but hadn't always known how to speak, I wouldn't have been surprised if the fire salamander had understood at least a few things.

Mostly the laptop appeared to hold agency files, including some reports that referred to incidents with me.

"A quick search for your name showed three or four, and then I put in 'fire salamander' too. Jacobs didn't get me anything, though."

"Not surprised by that," I said. No way Jacobs would have been referred to by name by the sound of how things had been run. He was too far up the chain of command compared to Crawley.

I tried not to panic as I read my old files and saw information on me I'd not known for sure they had. But I'd suspected they had it, and I kept telling myself that it didn't matter now. I'd been featured on every major news network across the globe. People knew far more about me now than they ever had. News helicopters regularly flew over, trying to get a glimpse of Zephyr and me as we went flying, and there were photos of my face everywhere.

Taking a couple of deep breaths, I let Erlan guide me onward.

"The part that puzzled me most," he said a moment later, "was this."

He clicked through to what looked like a forum or chat area in the agency's systems.

"She seems to have added an agent to her work area since you shut down the agency building here in LA. And there's a meeting between this new agent and her."

"A meeting?"

"Yes. A recurring one. At a small beachside cafe. With an Agent Dagraza."

I lifted both eyebrows.

Did he just say Agent Dagraza? Zephyr asked.

I nodded.

That's Azargad backward.

"That meeting is for Zephyr and me," I said aloud a moment later.

"Oh, wow. That's..."

"She must have known we'd hack her laptop eventually." I ran a hand through my hair, excited and nervous. Crawley had reached out to me. But why?

"Well, the next one is scheduled for three hours from now," Erlan pointed out. "And it's not too far from where you fly regularly.

"And just after dark." I hastily memorized the details, telling them to Zephyr as I got up and handed the laptop back to Erlan.

"Thanks, Erlan. You've been awesome. But I've got somewhere to be, and I think Minsheng is going to want to know about it."

Getting up, I gave Newton a head rub and patted Erlan on the shoulder. I was more than a little grateful the young elf had decided to join us.

"Have fun persuading him to let you go," Erlan replied.

I chuckled as Zephyr led the way back down to the main warehouse floor. I'd manage it somehow. It wasn't as if he could stop me, but I knew he would have an opinion that would be valuable. And after all, he was still my Shishou.

We found the man getting the training area ready for me and Erlan.

"Absolutely not," Minsheng said the moment I finished telling him. "It's almost guaranteed to be a trap."

"Is it? Crawley's probably been fired," I replied. "And she knows I've got this laptop. I'm the only person who can even see this meeting exists. Well, me and Erlan."

Minsheng frowned.

"She wants you to meet her?"

"Yup. And I think I know why."

"You do?" Daisy asked, making it clear she'd heard the whole thing despite only now stepping out of one of the large equipment cabinets.

"The agent who tried to take the orb from Ronan and me. I think they were either related to Crawley or it was Crawley."

My words were met with silence, and for a second, I thought they had all decided I was crazy.

"You're sure of that, aren't you?" Minsheng said a moment later, looking more thoughtful.

"No, but they were familiar, and I think they could have

killed Ronan if they'd wanted to. Both of us were blind-sided. I think she's trying to get to the Sanctuary. I'm also pretty sure the bike she rode off on had been in the parking lot under the agency building, but I didn't want to say until I heard this."

"That doesn't explain what she wants with you."

"No, but when I first met her, she decided to be compassionate and risked her entire career on letting me go. In my experience, people make decisions based on their emotions. Something about Zephyr and me made her sympathetic. And now she's looking for the Sanctuary too. What if she knows another mythical? Or has let another mythical go in the past?"

"It's possible. I knew you could be persuasive but it would make how she reacted to you more justifiable and also explain why Knox was the one who followed us across the entire country." Minsheng sighed.

"But you still don't like the idea of me meeting her?" I replied, coming closer. Although I didn't want to have to badger him until he gave his consent, I did want this consent, and I wanted him to feel listened to.

"I don't like the idea of you being in trouble at any point, but we're in the dark here. We've got an unknown enemy in an unknown place. Orbs are going missing and being destroyed by an unknown force and for unknown reasons, and she's the only person who can give us some answers."

"Then I guess we'd best put a plan together and do some training because Zephyr and I have a meeting to go to."

This seemed to spur everyone on, and within twenty minutes, Daisy and Minsheng had scurried off to get some stuff ready. They were going to be our backup, although they wouldn't be our transport. There wasn't anything big enough to transport us now anyway, so we were going to need to fly in, but if Minsheng and Daisy had made sure it was safe first, we'd be minimizing our risk.

That meant Zephyr and I could practice whatever we wanted.

No sooner had I thought this than Zephyr exhaled slowly toward the middle of the room, white gas pluming out in that direction.

I growled at the lack of warning but reached for the particles with my mind. They resisted my control, especially as I reached farther in, almost as if they were a living entity pushing back against my will.

Despite that, I managed to harness the technique I'd been honing to form the gas into a ball. Moving the ball was another matter, and trying made my head hurt.

Slowly, I managed to lift it higher, making the dojo and sparring area safe again for the lessons Lyra would teach a little later. Zephyr opened his mouth to do the same thing again, but I reached out for him and shook my head.

Sorry, buddy. That's about all I've got in the tank unless we can eat some more and take a break. That was not easy.

He sighed and rolled his eyes but grinned a moment later.

Pizza?

I laughed and nodded. Why not pizza? After all, we'd want to be well fed if we were going out into the dangerous world to meet an undercover agent.

The moment I thought of it, I couldn't help but wonder if we'd find Crawley injured or if she'd be fine. Had it been her sneaking through that woods to get to the orb, or was I seeing connections that weren't there? It was only a matter of time before we found out.

CHAPTER EIGHT

As the last customer made their way out of the cafe, I started to wonder if this had been a setup or if the meeting had been a one-off and I'd missed it. Or all sorts of other possible reasons why after waiting in the fading light of the evening, I'd still not seen Crawley anywhere.

Zephyr was sitting in the shadows between two cars in the parking lot, but it was now dark enough that he could consider moving closer.

Daisy and Minsheng were farther away but still in the parking lot and armed to the teeth. I wasn't comfortable with the latter, but I wanted them to be able to defend themselves, if nothing else.

Before long, Zephyr joined me, his company reassuring. Despite that, I was ready to leave.

I was partway through thinking it when a woman with a large overcoat on came walking up the beach. She was keeping to the shadows and looked over her shoulder more than once.

A couple of times, I thought she stared my way as if she

thought she saw something in the gloom and was considering coming closer.

I stepped into a lighter patch, the cafe no longer shielding me from a nearby streetlamp. Her eyes fixed on me and she changed direction, heading straight toward me.

Once more she glanced over her shoulder, and I backtracked into the shadow.

Looks like we're in luck, I told Zephyr.

Her turning up is a start, but she'd better have answers.

If she's awkward, we can always gas her and take her back to the warehouse.

You think she'll be more likely to talk?

No, probably not.

May be best to not make abduction our style, then. As appealing as it is to use their own tactics on them.

I sighed as if I were annoyed that he was spoiling my fun, but he had a point. We probably shouldn't be joking about abducting people, given what the agency had been doing for years.

Crawley came right into the shadows as if she had nothing to fear or to lose. I wasn't sure which, but I wasn't going to display any fear either.

"How's the arm?" I asked immediately.

It caught her off-guard, but the surprise in her eyes made me pretty sure I'd guessed correctly. There was silence while I waited to see if she'd confirm or deny it.

"Had no idea you were even there until you knocked that gun out of my hands. Didn't realize that centaur was yours," she eventually said.

"He's not mine. And he's okay, by the way."

"Good. I didn't want to hurt him, but that was the fifth

orb I'd turned up to find, only for it to be gone, broken, or have someone guarding it."

"So, you're desperate for an orb. Why? Do you have mythical blood in you?" I asked, knowing I sounded a lot more pissed off than I was.

"No," she said, snapping the word far too fast.

"Then you wouldn't have been able to activate it. You know that, right? You need mythical blood, DNA or whatever, to get it to work. They're useless to you, but not to the people who need them to get to safety."

"Oh," she said, gulping.

"Is that why you wanted to meet me? To get me to give you an orb or tell you where the Sanctuary is? Because I won't do either."

She shook her head.

I paused, the anger I'd felt suddenly leaving me. If she didn't want me here to ask for an orb, then why had she come? And what was so important about getting to the Sanctuary?

"I know we've not agreed on many things, but I'm hoping you can help me."

"Then you'd best spit it out because I've got mythicals to protect and an orb thief to track down."

Her eyes widened.

"It's not you destroying the orbs?" she asked a moment later.

"How could it be? I wouldn't leave mythicals stranded like that. The Sanctuary is still a haven for many." I left out everything else I thought.

"Then..." She shook her head. "It doesn't matter now. I need you to help my daughter."

"Your daughter?"

"She's half-mythical. I fell in love with an elf. Had no idea that's what he was until much later. Anyway. We had a kid, and then he left. When an agent showed up for him, he just abandoned us. I vowed I'd never let another mythical do that. He deceived us and then left me high and dry."

"So, you've hunted mythicals ever since?" I asked, my anger rising.

"I had to beg and plead with those agents not to harm my daughter. They let me keep her on one condition: that I work for them. I'd already worked for a tracing program that looked for missing people. I had the skills they needed, and the agreement worked. Until you came along." Crawley paused, shaking her head and sighing. "You look so much like her, and when you asked me to let you live, I knew I'd want an agent to make the same decision for my daughter when I was gone."

I exhaled, not sure what to do with the revelations. She had an elven daughter. But where was that girl now, and how could I help her? Rather than making any more demands of Crawley, I opted to stay quiet and let her talk. It seemed there was far more to this story than I'd realized.

"When you made everything public, I thought it was finally all over. Jacobs didn't give up, of course. Ordered me to do everything I could to kill you, and he clearly didn't like it that I didn't. You interrupted him threatening me. He didn't confirm it, but he implied he knew about my daughter."

"And he shouldn't have?" I asked, knowing where this was going.

"No. But when you came in and had overpowered

everyone, I thought that was it. Thought we were finally safe. Emily didn't agree. She said she didn't feel safe, but she had heard of a place that was, not that she told me what place she meant."

"The Sanctuary?"

"I believe so."

"How did you hear about it?" I asked. "Knox?"

"He mentioned that you'd fled somewhere that magic kept hidden, but I had to go digging to find his reports. I did, and I put two and two together."

"So you want me to check if your daughter's there?"

"I'm not sure she made it, but I think she was looking for it. Her apartment has been ransacked, and she's gone." Crawley gulped again and I finally noticed her wringing her hands. I was standing before a mother who was worried sick about her kid—someone who just wanted her daughter to be safe.

"I'll do what I can. I'll start at the Sanctuary and see if she made it. Some mythicals are still managing to find orbs and get through. If she didn't, I'll see if I can find her. But I'm likely to need your help. What do you know about Jacobs?"

"He's not going to let this rest, and he's not going to play fair. He's got more weight with the government than I do. It was like there was an endless budget for anything he thought necessary."

"He's powerful and pissed off; we knew that already," I replied, my feet starting to hurt from standing so long. "What can you tell us about where he is and what his next moves are likely to be?"

"I don't know where he operates from, and I definitely

don't know where he lives. He was rarely in one place and not always in the US. You have to understand, he was above my pay grade. That's why I've come to you. I've got nothing, and unofficially, I'm not even employed anymore." She looked up at Zephyr, who was still towering beside me, trying to look intimidating.

"Unofficially?"

"We're on hold. Something about a reshuffle and re-mandate."

"All right," I said. "We're not going to make any more progress here like this. I'll look for your daughter because she's a mythical and make sure she gets safely to the Sanctuary. That's all I'll promise."

"That's all I could hope for. I just want her somewhere safe." Crawley nodded and then looked around again. Her posture changed, and she looked like she was about to bolt.

"I've got to go," she said.

I looked over her shoulder and tried to see whatever she had, but I wasn't sure what had spooked her. It was clear she didn't want to be here any longer, however.

"I'll reach out when I have something," I said, turning to Zephyr.

Let's go, buddy.

He flew up at the same time I pushed up with my powers, and both of us launched into the air.

That was unexpected, he replied as soon as we were together in the air and I was riding on his back again.

You're telling me. But it explains a lot.

Again, I looked in the direction Crawley had taken off and where she'd seemed to spot something, but I could only see a small yacht out at sea and little else. Whatever had made her think it was time to go, it was something known only to her.

We should help her daughter, but it doesn't sound good, Zephyr replied.

I frowned as Zephyr flew low toward the car with Daisy and Minsheng. I caught sight of our Shishou and saw the relief on his face.

No, I don't think she's at the Sanctuary, I thought as I gave a big thumbs-up to let Minsheng know we were good and heading back to the dojo. *And we've got Jacobs to deal with, and whatever is happening to these orbs.*

We're not going to get bored.

No, definitely not.

I sighed as we flew back toward the dojo. Part of me didn't want to go back. There was so much responsibility. The building needed to be extended, and I had to work out what was happening to the Sanctuary's orbs. They hadn't asked me to, but I couldn't rest if I didn't get to the bottom of it. And now Crawley's daughter.

While I knew Jacobs was probably involved in a lot of it, I wasn't completely sure he would have the half-elf, or if something else might have happened to her. It was possible whoever originally agreed to Crawley's terms of employment had been after her. Or many other people. It was also still possible she was on her way to the Sanctuary.

Although flying with Zephyr normally helped me clear my head, I had too many things to think about this time, and by the time Zephyr landed on the roof and we walked into the temporary shelter and bedrooms we'd built on top, I couldn't help but wonder if life was ever going to feel simple again.

Immediately I went to find Erlan. He was poring over his new laptop again.

"You need something?" he asked when I handed him Crawley's old device.

"Her daughter is missing. I need everything you can find out about her. She's a half-elf, and she might be in trouble. Name's Emily."

Erlan's eyes went wide, but he took the laptop and nodded.

"I know it's not something you're used to doing, but you're clearly good at this stuff. When you're not doing that, keep training. I think we're further from done with the agency than we hoped."

"Yeah, I was beginning to worry about that, especially after the news report Chris had on."

I lifted my eyebrows and opened my mouth to ask Erlan to explain, but I closed it again before I could utter my request. I could go find out what he meant myself. It wouldn't be much slower and it would mean I had first-hand knowledge. I'd never liked just having someone tell me what I'd missed.

Chris was at the table in the kitchen, eating a late-night snack with his laptop open when Zephyr and I found him.

After sticking a couple of pizzas in the oven for Zephyr and grabbing some chips and a soda for me, I plonked down beside him. Before I could ask Chris to show me what Erlan had been talking about, Daisy and Minsheng appeared.

Instead of getting to ask the questions, for the next few minutes I had to answer them, letting my mentor and his sister know what had happened with Crawley. It had the added benefit of filling Chris in and making the time while Zephyr waited for his pizzas go quickly.

"You know you're supposed to be taking care of your dragon, not feeding him junk food," Chris said when I dumped both of them on a large platter and stuck it on the kitchen counter so Zephyr didn't have to bend down so far to eat it.

"He gets pizza after a mission, especially a late-night one. That's our deal for making him miss his beauty sleep," I replied. It had become a thing, and I wasn't about to stop it, even if I did sometimes cheat and used frozen pizzas rather than spending loads of money on takeout ones.

"Well, before you two decide you're done for the night, I think the agency is making a move. A government representative was doing one of those political talk shows this evening. Made a point of saying how much danger mythicals posed and how someone should oversee our roles in society and make sure we're not using our abilities and magic to influence things unfairly in our favor."

I sighed. It wasn't that people suggesting we were dangerous was new. Normal people had been doing it since we went public. But a government type? That meant they were making a move to get political support for something.

"So what you're telling me is we need a PR person to start showing people that mythicals make the world better, not worse, and we're really friendly?" I replied.

Chris chuckled but nodded.

"And by PR person, we all mean you. You're the face everyone trusts, and they're all fascinated with Zephyr. If they can be made to believe the large and scary-looking dragon is safe, then we've already won half the battle." Chris sat back, looking at Minsheng and me.

Minsheng nodded, and I sighed again. I didn't have any desire to be on the news again.

"We'll get something set up," Daisy said. "And we'll keep looking into ways to expand this place. Anyway. Time to sleep and face it all tomorrow."

"I don't feel like I can sleep with Crawley's daughter missing," I said, voicing the thought as it came into my head.

"You said she'd been missing a while?" Daisy replied as the others tidied up and Zephyr finished eating.

"Crawley implied it had been at least two weeks already." I frowned. It was a long time for a person to be missing.

"Then a few more hours is highly unlikely to make much difference. Until we get a lead, we can't do a lot."

I nodded, grateful for friends with wise counsel. I promised myself I'd go to her apartment and find out what I could in the morning. Between Erlan, Zephyr, and me, hopefully, we could find something to work with.

CHAPTER NINE

Sleeping on your problems didn't always help. All night I tossed and turned beside Zephyr, earning me disapproving grunts and flicks of his tail.

Now that I knew Emily was part-elf and possibly in danger, I couldn't shake the idea that I should be doing everything I could to find her, but there were so many other needs. It was clear I was going to have to go on TV again and try to calm public fears about mythicals. Holfin, the dwarf we'd helped, was now staying with us because he felt safer here than at his apartment. Although I suspected his budding romantic interest to be a factor, he'd had some good points about how his neighbors had been treating him.

On top of that, I was worried about the orbs, Jacobs, Crawley, and what I was going to do about the Sanctuary and the mixed reactions I'd received the last time I was there.

As I was getting dressed, I noticed the plant pot I still had. It was full of dirt, and I'd been watering it a little each day. The seed inside had begun to grow, although the only thing visible was the top of a bent-over stalk and the first sign of a leaf. The water master in the Sanctuary had given it to me when I'd asked him if it was possible I might be able to control more than one element.

So far, no luck. But I hadn't tried recently, and I wasn't going to get to try today despite assuring the water master I wouldn't give up.

"Sorry," I whispered as I pulled my socks on and got up.

Zephyr tilted his head to the side but didn't say anything. Instead, the two of us made our way to breakfast. We'd already agreed that our trip to the apartment would take place as soon as we'd eaten. My abilities drained my body of energy quickly, and Zephyr was almost always hungry. Neither of us was going anywhere on an empty stomach. It was a recipe for disaster.

We'd only been at the table eating for a minute or two when Minsheng hurried in.

"Oh, good. I'm glad you're both here. I've just gotten off the phone with the organization about funding us to add bedrooms on the roof."

I lifted my eyebrows.

"Daisy's idea," Minsheng explained. "They're not against the concept. They want to see the building, however, and they also mentioned that it was past time for them to finally give you your official introduction interview and trials."

"My what?" I asked.

"You and Zephyr, actually. They want to interview you and get you to do the introduction trials." Minsheng swallowed as if he knew I wasn't going to be happy about that.

"But you've been my Shishou for about six months. Isn't it a bit late for introductions? What are they going to do, ask me to put Zephyr back in his egg and go home?"

This made Minsheng chuckle, but he shook his head.

"I know it's out of the blue, but I think if things had been calmer and we hadn't spent so much time fighting agents, on the run, and generally making things difficult for the organization, they'd have sent someone already."

"And let me guess, I need to pass these trials?"

"Sort of, yes. I don't think they're going to be very difficult, but they'll want you to do well at them. Also, if we're to secure funding, it's a pretty important thing for them to be happy." Minsheng gave me what looked like an apologetic smile.

They'll be impressed, Zephyr said in my head. I knew he was trying to reassure me, but I wasn't so sure. And I didn't like the idea of trials.

I was going to have to put it out of my head, though. We had someone to find, and I couldn't be any later.

You ready to go find Crawley's daughter? I asked a moment later.

Definitely ready to try. But this is a big country, and we have no idea if she was taken or left of her own accord.

No, but I really hope it wasn't that first one.

We'll find her either way. We've not failed at anything yet. Zephyr's eyes met mine and I gave him a brief nod, grateful for his faith in us. I had no idea how much he now remembered of his dragon ancestors' lives, but with each week that passed, he grew stronger and more resilient and even wiser. While it was a little strange, I was regularly thankful for all he was capable of.

As soon as we were in the air, I felt better. Heading somewhere with one task in mind allowed me to momentarily leave all the other worries behind me. I couldn't do more than one task at once, and there was little point worrying about challenges I wasn't going to have to face yet. It could be months before the organization sent someone to interview us. At least weeks.

Although Crawley hadn't given us her daughter's address, Erlan had provided it and what little he knew. Her bills were still being paid; it looked like her mother had deposited money into Emily's accounts to ensure this. She'd also been to the apartment recently and listened to the answering machine. Something not many people had these days.

Other than that, Emily wasn't reported missing and no one else had asked where she was. Which meant she didn't have any friends, or they were with her, or some other third possible scenario I wasn't sure of yet.

I had Erlan trying to work out if there was anyone close to her who might know anything, but I was still hoping that I wouldn't need to involve lots of other people. Crawley clearly didn't want others to know too much.

Zephyr landed on the roof of the apartment house and I sighed. He wasn't going to fit into the building.

Sorry, buddy. Guess they didn't know you were coming to poke around.

One day everything will be big enough for a dragon, he replied, sitting and then lying himself down near the door. *But for now, you'll have to go on without me.*

I'll describe it to you, I said as I pulled open the door, surprised to find it unlocked. I guess most people weren't expecting visitors to fly in, and the apartment complex was far enough away from nearby buildings it wasn't as if anyone could jump across. The fire escape also appeared to be internal and the building fairly new.

A lot of apartments in LA had been converted from large old houses or warehouses and had fire escapes on the outside. This must have been a much more expensive place to live. Had Crawley been funding her daughter, or was Emily successful in the human world?

I knew Erlan was likely to be able to answer that question, so I hurried down, looking for the apartment number Erlan had supplied. When I reached a door with a fifteen on it in gold writing, I stopped.

Pulling a small toolset out of my backpack, I crouched in front of the door. The lockpicks were part of a set Chris owned. He'd given me permission to use them when needed and had shown me how to use them, but it was a while since I'd practiced, and I'd not been very good. I would just have to do my best, however.

It took me several minutes and several explanations to Zephyr about why I wasn't giving him any more information. It seemed to irritate him that I wasn't already inside.

When I did finally get the door unlocked, I gave myself a little cheer and put the tools away.

Going in, I finally told Zephyr and pushed the door open.

It swung inward to reveal a tidy hallway with coat hooks on the wall opposite the door. There wasn't much hung from them, and I was sure that someone had taken something. It had that look to it that the lower clothes get when they've had the weight of larger coats and bags on top of them. Sort of squashed, but not completely.

Once I'd noticed that, I walked around the corner into the rest of the hallway. There was a pile of mail on a small table in the corner, and that was where the neatness ended. I could see into a small bedroom, and it was a mess. Clothes, makeup, and bedroom furniture were scattered everywhere. Draws had been dumped out, and the mattress had been slashed.

I had no way of knowing if the person searching had found what they were looking for, but they'd clearly not cared about the contents of the room nor put anything back. I moved on, wanting to check everything before I reached for Zephyr to discuss what could have happened.

The bathroom was more intact, but a small storage unit by the toilet had been upended into the bathtub and the side panel had been ripped off the clean white cabinet. Again, someone had been hunting for something.

I noticed there was no toothbrush anywhere. That was an encouraging sign. If there was no toothbrush, Emily might have left before the place was trashed like this.

I tried to take in as much of what I saw as possible in case something turned out to be relevant later. I took my time looking at everything and estimating how long it had been like this. The showerhead had been dripping on the roll of toilet paper in the bottom of the bathtub, turning it into a pulpy mess that took me a moment to recognize, so I'd have said it wasn't a recent situation.

I moved into the only other room in the apartment, a reasonable-sized kitchen and living area. Once again, all the drawers, cabinets, and storage units had been emptied and searched, and the cushions had been slashed, stuffing partially pulled out. Someone had clearly made a path through it, the wreckage pushed to the sides of a narrow walkway from the door to the kitchen sink.

For a moment, I didn't move. I tried to imagine what this would have felt like for Emily to have come back to if she'd not left before it happened. Could this have made her run? Had she already been heading to the Sanctuary? Or had this happened after she'd been captured? I still had no way to know, especially since that Crawley had been in here since as well.

The path could easily have been cleared by Crawley, by whoever trashed the place, or by Emily.

I stepped farther in and took more of the room in. The kitchen looked to be less broken and destroyed, and I wasn't sure why at first. It seemed like they'd spared the glasses and dishes and pots and pans.

It looked like they'd been moved around, and some packages of food had been pulled out of a cupboard, but I could walk into the kitchen without being in danger of kicking evidence across the floor.

Trying not to worry about who could have done this, I went to the fridge, one of the only things that was shut, and opened it. There was very little in there, a few bottles and jars of sauces that kept for weeks and a tub of butter. It was possible Emily didn't keep much in her house, or she'd cleared the last of her food out before she left, but Crawley might also have emptied out anything that would go bad.

Coupled with the missing toothbrush, it gave me a stronger indication, however, and it served to ease my nerves a little. Although I couldn't be sure, it was looking like Emily had left her apartment herself. If she was hiding from whoever did this, she might be fine and just unable to contact her mother to let her know. That would be the most welcome scenario.

Something about it didn't sit right, however. It was clear Emily was in danger even if she was safe for now. But why? Crawley had defied her orders months ago and let me live. Why was someone after Emily now? To punish Crawley?

I didn't know the answer, and I needed another mind to help me try to work it out. I took my time going over everything again and telling Zephyr about it while he waited above.

What do you think, buddy? I asked when I stood by the door again, none the wiser.

Have you listened to her messages or looked through her mail? They might hold some clues.

I sighed, surprised I'd forgotten both of those but grateful that Zephyr hadn't. A moment later, I was back by the little answering machine and pressing play. There weren't many messages, and some of them were from people trying to sell stuff or scam, but one stuck out. I played it twice to be sure.

"Hey, Em," a cheery female voice said. "I know you're not back from your trip yet, but I couldn't wait to tell you that Eddy asked the big question finally. You have to be a bridesmaid. Call me as soon as you come through that door."

I grinned at the enthusiasm and excitement in that voice for so many reasons. Not only did Emily have a friend, but she'd clearly told said friend that she was going somewhere for a while and wouldn't be able to communicate any other way. It made me feel a little calmer about her current predicament. Now I just needed to figure out where she'd gone.

I kept listening to calls that were less helpful as I picked up the small stack of mail. Some had already been opened, and I was pretty sure Crawley had been thinking along similar lines, but other than some bills she'd paid and a bunch of ads I doubted Emily needed right now, there was nothing to make me any wiser.

After putting everything back the way I'd found it, I made my way up to the roof and Zephyr. We talked some more as we flew up into the LA sky. The situation was clear. We had no leads, but Emily was probably hiding somewhere.

For now, I needed to keep Erlan looking for her and hope for the best. Especially with everything else I also had to sort out.

CHAPTER TEN

"Nicely done," Minsheng said as I showed him what Zephyr and I could now do with the gas he exhaled.

It had taken me a few more attempts and some modifications in the way Zephyr spread the gas, but we had a system where he could make me a small cloud of gas and I could move it where we needed it to go.

The process took a lot of my concentration, and I still wasn't ready to do it in battle, but I could think of a few situations where it would be useful. Assuming we got into more fights.

"Why don't you take a break and have a snack? I've got to call the organization again about this meeting. They want some details about the warehouse." He smiled as he looked at his phone and pulled up his to-do list. "Oh, and in an hour, there's a news link interview for you to do. They want to stream you and Zephyr into their studio and interview you over the internet or something." Minsheng walked away as he spoke, and I sighed.

I didn't want to do an interview, but I had promised I

would try to counter the suggestions the government was putting out about us being dangerous. Although I wasn't sure I could do masses to combat that fear, I opted to take the call out on the roof with Zephyr alongside me. He'd even agreed to talk so people could see he wasn't a mindless beast.

Previously, I'd done most of the talking, but I'd begun wondering if that might have been a mistake. Everyone was scared of Zephyr and what the other mythical creatures could do, and the elves, dwarves, gnomes, and other humanoid races had been caught up in the same fear. It was a difficult thing to navigate.

I'd known it wouldn't be easy to bring the world to a place where they would accept that we just wanted to live alongside them. There was enough racial hatred and strife over human differences to make it clear it would take some time to accept mythicals. I'd just hoped there would be enough people who had always dreamed of mythical creatures and races who would embrace us.

After taking a quick break with Zephyr, getting some snacks, and making sure I was at least vaguely presentable, we made our way up to the roof. It was an overcast day, but in case the sun came out, we were underneath a dome of canvas big enough for Zephyr to sit comfortably.

I found Daisy up there arranging the chairs and the camera to try to get it looking right.

"I really wish we didn't have to do things like this," I said as I slipped into the chair and tried to look relaxed.

"Tell me about it, but if anyone can make us look like we're less of a threat, you can. You've been great in the past. Just keep calm and be yourself."

I looked at Zephyr as he tried to get comfortable. Neither of us said anything. We didn't need to. He didn't really want to be doing this either, but it had to be done.

At least, staying silent didn't seem like the right way to handle it, and the media were always hungry to interview us.

I checked that the air barrier I usually created was set around me and tried to relax, but my hands shook, and I couldn't keep still.

Daisy helped me to calm, handed me a bottle of water, and then warned me when the feed was about to start. Immediately we could hear our interviewer and see her on the screen. Daisy stood behind, giving me a thumbs-up and encouraging me to smile.

Although I didn't feel like smiling as the interviewer talked and worked up to the first question, I did my best to appear calm.

"I understand that you've turned your building into a dojo, Aella-Faye. Have you always embraced being able to instruct people in martial arts?" the host eventually asked.

"It's always been a passion of mine to help people learn and grow, and also help themselves feel safer and as if they can defend themselves, so I predominantly taught women. I don't teach many classes currently, but occasionally help my friend who uses this building for her dojo."

"But the building is in your name?"

"Correct," I replied, feeling and sounding like I was on trial.

"So you have friends around you who are heavily involved in the martial arts?"

"It's been really lovely having the classes here," I said,

not sure where this conversation was going but deciding to take it in another direction. "All sorts of people come to learn here and go away feeling safer. It's just one way we give back to the community in LA and try to make this city safer for everyone in it."

"And what does your dragon do while you're teaching?" she asked.

"Oh, Zephyr, here? He can talk. He's fully sentient. Why don't we let him answer that question himself?" I leaned sideways and kept my smile on my face. They'd assured us that Zephyr would be treated with respect, but it didn't seem like that so far.

Zephyr tilted his head lower, bringing it closer to me. To be fair, it looked a little intimidating if you didn't know he was perfectly friendly, but hopefully, we were about to prove that.

"I do a variety of things." Zephyr's voice sounded strange when it came out of his mouth when I was used to hearing him in my head, but we were keeping that capability to ourselves for now. "I don't like to be in an enclosed space for very long, so I sometimes fly into a larger space in the building that suits me better. At other times I will assist in teaching some of the mythicals here. Not all of them can speak English, so I translate."

"You translate for other mythical people, such as dwarves and elves?"

"No, I translate for the mythicals that elves can form a unique bond with, such as fire salamanders."

"Fire salamanders?" Our interviewer's eyebrows rose, but her face quickly returned to normal.

"Yes, they're like normal salamanders mostly," I replied

and tried to smile. "Except, just as their name suggests, they can create a fire when scared or threatened. We teach them to control that and create a safe place for them to practice. While the secret agency was trying to make us disappear, some of them came to our rescue, and we took them in and helped keep them safe in return."

"That sounds fascinating."

"It's definitely never dull."

The interviewer paused, clearly flustered by the information we'd given her, before launching into the next question.

"There have been concerns raised by people in the last few weeks over the safety of humans when nearby or meeting with different creatures and races. You seem to be a sort of spokesperson for the mythicals, as you call them. Do you ensure they're all abiding by the law as well as being protected themselves?"

The question was clearly loaded, and I wasn't sure how to answer it.

"I have very few mythicals at the dojo with me, but none of them have broken the law unless you count our altercations with the agency that has been hunting us—and I'm sure you'll agree that was self-defense. We never instigated a fight. I can't speak for any mythicals outside of my small circle, though. There are many more, and at least one large group I know of who deliberately limited all connections with humanity out of fear of their own safety. Many of them continue to do so."

"So no one polices them?"

"They police themselves. They have councils and societal structures like any normal civilization."

"So nothing stops them from committing crimes?"

"Their consciences stop them, as it does most humans. They're not society-less. But also, fear has stopped them. You have to understand. Until I defeated the agency here in LA, they hid from humanity *all* the time. They've not been committing any crimes. They've just been hiding as best they could."

"And now? They're not hiding now."

I frowned, trying to think of a good response. It was clearly a fear that was going to be played on by the media.

"Most are still hiding and living where they were. Some have come to stay with me," I replied, buying time for my mind to catch up. "Every mythical I've met wants what the average human wants—to be able to live their life in safety and peace. Those who live in the US would love to be considered citizens. They want to live by the same ethics and achieve the American dream."

Daisy gave me a thumbs-up and motioned toward the door as if she were going to get something. I didn't understand all the gestures, but I had to shift my focus back to my interviewer when she directly asked Zephyr a question about flying.

He started to answer, but partway through, he stopped.

"Shooter," he yelled before diving toward me, but his words came too late for me to dodge.

A bullet struck the air barrier I'd created around me and slowed, giving Zephyr time to get his head and body down over me. It pinged off his scales and hit the concrete floor.

We both got to our feet. I tried to see where it had come from as Zephyr launched into the air.

Our interview forgotten, I forced the air behind me and downward, propelling myself after Zephyr. The dragon was flying so fast that I struggled to keep up, let alone catch up.

Movement on the roof of another building drew my attention. It was far enough away that I hadn't considered it a danger, but clearly I'd been wrong. The sniper ran, his gun dismantled and on his shoulder as Zephyr came closer.

The would-be assassin rushed toward a door on the roof and tried to pull it open. I hurled it shut again with as much wind as I could manage, almost overbalancing myself as I kept the pressure up.

Zephyr flew closer, trying to get there while I delayed the sniper.

Caught in the windstream I was creating, the guy struggled to get away from the door, having given up on opening it. He moved out of the blast and ran across the roof.

I tried to use my air to keep the guy pinned down, but the force I needed to keep myself flying as well was making me feel exhausted. I tried to get closer, hoping Zephyr could catch him.

When the man realized he wasn't getting away, he stopped, pulled a smaller gun from somewhere, and opened fire. At first he targeted Zephyr, and the bullets ricocheted in all directions.

When he realized that wasn't going to work and Zephyr was almost upon him, he turned the gun on me. I blasted myself up and pushed more air ahead to make myself harder to hit.

The assassin fired until the gun was empty. A moment

later, Zephyr descended upon him, both claws grabbing arms and pulling the sniper into the air.

Head back to our dojo and get the others to come help, Zephyr said.

I let myself fall in a more controlled manner toward the warehouse, hoping the shooter couldn't get any more shots off from where he was.

I landed as Zephyr swooped overhead, and then I ran for the stairs, calling for Daisy, Chris and Minsheng.

"Sniper tried to kill us. Zephyr's got him," I called down the stairs as I heard the commotion of people running upstairs to the roof.

Incoming, Zephyr said into my head. I looked up to see where he was, following his movements as he flew over to the roof.

Daisy was the first to arrive, carrying a dart gun in one hand and some zip ties in the other. She ran past me, looking for the threat. Behind her were Minsheng and Chris, both of them strapping on Kevlar vests.

I tried not to panic as Zephyr landed with the sniper. We'd been up against gunmen before, but it was clear this one was a good shot. Reaching for the air around us, I waited to use it if I needed to.

Daisy didn't hesitate, however, and shot at the vulnerable man. A moment later, a set of feathers stuck out of his chest, and he went limp. I rushed over to help her catch him and get him on the roof more gently as Zephyr let him go.

"What on earth happened?" Minsheng asked as he got close, a dart gun in his hands as well.

"This guy tried to shoot me. Zephyr got in the way just

in time," I replied, not adding that I'd slowed the bullet with my wall of air. It hadn't been enough, but I didn't want anyone to realize I could defend myself that way just yet.

Chris and Daisy banded the man's wrists and ankles together with zip ties and patted him down for weapons. A moment later, he was restrained and out cold. Only as I straightened and ran a hand through my hair did I remember the camera had been active and I'd been in the middle of an interview.

I turned to the camera we'd performed this last part in front of and the laptop beside that showed me the feed and the host. She was still there, and we were still live. I gulped.

The world had just heard Zephyr and me defend ourselves against a sniper and then seen Daisy shoot our attacker. Given the questions we'd been asked, I was pretty sure this wasn't a good thing.

As the others grabbed the guy's arms and legs and carried him away, I moved closer to the camera and tried to block the scene.

"Sorry, everyone. It seems someone hired a sniper to try to kill us. As you can imagine, this is a scary situation to have to deal with. Thankfully we had some tranquilizer guns from the first time the agency hunted us, and the threat is sleeping the effects off. We'll be trying to work out who sent him when he's awake."

"Surely you should call the police and hand him over?" the hostess said, her face a little paler after all this.

I nodded without really thinking.

"As soon as we can, we'll get some help. Perhaps we can talk again soon. As you can probably imagine, now isn't a good time. I was lucky not to be hit and fortunate that Zephyr has scales hard enough to act like Kevlar, but this clearly isn't a safe place for us to be interviewed."

I reached forward as I finished speaking and cut the feed. It was an awful way to end the interview, but all things considered, I was grateful to be alive.

You okay? I asked Zephyr as I watched Chris, Minsheng, and Daisy manhandle the sniper down the stairs. They'd find somewhere to hold him until he woke up.

I'm going to have a few tender spots where those bullets struck me, but otherwise, I'm fine. Did you manage to slow that bullet?

Just about.

We got lucky, then.

I nodded, a shudder running up my spine. I'd not tried the shield in an actual combat situation. I'd done a massive wall during the last major battle with the agency, but that was fairly easy. It had been as thick as it needed to be. The shield around me needed to be thin and unobtrusive.

We'd got very lucky.

CHAPTER ELEVEN

I sat on the floor outside the cubicle we'd put our sniper in. His feet were just visible beneath the curtain, and it was obvious the guy was still out cold.

A moment later, Zephyr plonked down beside me. I leaned into him, appreciating his warm body and calming presence.

I'd been shaking for the last couple of minutes. This guy had almost killed me. If Zephyr hadn't noticed, I'd have been seriously injured, and although I'd expected it at some point, having it actually happen was a whole new level of scary.

No more being out in open spaces for too long, Zephyr said into my head.

But that just leads to us hiding and running again.

Until we find a way to neutralize this threat as well.

I sighed. I was tired of there being some kind of threat. I needed to find a victory that lasted more than a couple of weeks. We needed time to just be ourselves and relax instead of becoming heroes all the time.

"He'll be awake soon," Minsheng said, breaking into my thoughts. "I should talk to him. See if he'll say anything useful."

"No. We'll do it," I replied, getting to my feet. "We're who he came for. He might have more to say to us. And besides, if he doesn't tell me what I want to know, I'll have Zephyr fly him up really high and then let go. We'll see if I can catch him with my abilities."

Minsheng lifted his eyebrows and opened his mouth to respond, making me chuckle.

"Don't worry, that was a joke. I won't try to kill him. Might make him think I'm going to, though."

"Fair enough, I suppose. After all, he did just try to kill you."

Taking several deep breaths, I tried to calm down. I couldn't go in and talk to the sniper while I was on edge. I'd need to be calm and collected and watch for obvious signs of danger and telltale body language that might help me work out the truth. No pressure.

We can do this, Zephyr said, towering above me as we stood side by side.

I looked up at him and nodded. This was our moment to shine, and as always, we'd do it together.

Pushing back the curtain, I strode inside and made room for Zephyr. The area was only just large enough for the three of us. At first, the sniper didn't move.

I studied him for a moment, trying to figure out if he was still unconscious or pretending.

He's awake, Zephyr said in my head.

Let's get on with this, then, I replied.

I walked closer and tapped his leg with my foot.

"We know you're awake," I said. "So you might as well stop pretending."

He opened his eyes and looked at me. Then he looked at Zephyr, and I thought I saw a hint of fear.

"So, let's get straight to business. Who sent you? And why do they want us dead?"

"You're already aware I won't answer that question."

I tried to hide my annoyance. Part of me had hoped he'd cooperate.

"I did wonder if you'd say that. The thing is, you didn't get the job done. That means *your* life is now in danger, or you're about to spend a very long time in prison."

"The brief mentioned nothing about you being able to slow bullets or your scaly friend being bulletproof."

"Then you didn't do your homework. That entire fight I had with the agency was live, and we displayed both traits for everyone to see."

"What can I say? I don't watch much TV." The sniper shrugged.

"I don't care. Somebody sent you. Was it Jacobs?"

The sniper wouldn't meet my gaze, but I thought I saw a hint of recognition at the name.

"I don't like to assume things, but I'm pretty sure that was a yes. So, why don't you drop the act and tell me why he thought sending a sniper against me all alone was a good idea? Because he had to know you had no hope. Looks to me an awful lot like he just threw you under the bus."

The man's jaw clenched, and I was pretty sure I was getting to him. Still, he didn't speak.

I crouched to make it harder for him to avoid my gaze, and he finally looked at me.

"I don't want to hurt anyone. I just want to live and be left alone. I don't know why you do what you do, but I'd imagine you think you're doing good, if not for you, then for your country." I paused so my next statement would have more meaning. "I'm not a threat to your country."

"You can try to convince me to talk any way you like, but I swore to do a job, and I will keep my honor."

I stood up as I exhaled, trying not to show my frustration. This was going to be harder than I'd thought. I wondered if I should have let Minsheng do it instead.

Let me drop him off the roof, Zephyr said.

I told Minsheng we wouldn't do anything that violent.

Let me pretend to drop him off the roof then.

Sighing, I nodded. What did we have to lose at this point?

Zephyr moved quicker than I'd ever seen him. Almost effortlessly, he grabbed the man with one large paw and picked him up. The sniper wriggled, but Zephyr was far too strong for him to get away. Walking on three legs, Zephyr hurried toward the roof, leaving me to follow.

Once we were there, the would-be assassin seemed to understand what was about to happen. He began struggling all the more.

I watched Zephyr move to the edge of the roof and dangle him over. The sniper looked down, almost clinging to the dragon claw around his torso.

"This isn't a very friendly thing to do for someone who claims they just want peace."

"You tried to kill me without even thinking about who I

was and what I wanted. You call that friendly? And besides, I said I wanted to live, not that I wanted peace. Having you alive is threatening what I want."

While I spoke, Zephyr moved him farther out and then looked at me. This was the moment when we were going to get our answer or not.

"I'm going to ask you one last time. Who do you work for, and why do they want us dead?"

The sniper looked down, perturbed by his predicament. But when he looked at me, his eyes were full of steel and resolve. He wasn't going to be intimidated.

"There you are," Minsheng said. "I've been looking all over for you."

I frowned. He'd known I was interrogating our prisoner. But then I noticed who was with him. Another stranger, this one a woman getting toward retirement by her appearance.

As I assessed her, she assessed me.

She wore a gray pencil skirt and a white blouse, and she had a clipboard in her hands and reading glasses on her face. She wore them in that awkward place, a little too far down her nose. It gave her a look of superiority as she surveyed me over the top of them.

A deep tangle formed in the pit of my stomach. She was here to decide if something was okay or not; I could tell.

There was only one place she could be from: the organization. That meant I was probably already in trouble.

"I'm Aella," I said. "I was just finishing up here, and then I'm sure we can talk about whatever you'd like to."

Does that mean our interrogation is over? Zephyr asked me.

Afraid so. I don't think he was going to talk anyway.

Zephyr brought the sniper back in from the edge but didn't set him on his feet.

I'll take him back down to the cubicle and get Daisy or Chris to hand him over to the police.

Sounds like a plan. Come back as soon as you can. I have a feeling we're going to need to explain ourselves.

I'm sure we can get her to like us. Or bribe her with Daisy's cooking.

I felt the corner of my mouth twitch up as I tried not to laugh at Zephyr's idea. Daisy's cooking wasn't a bad idea. She was a phenomenal chef, and since the occupants of the building had been growing, she'd taken it upon herself to make sure we weren't just fed well but with a great variety of wonderful foods.

"Is something amusing?" the new woman asked. Her accent threw me; it was upper-class British, the kind you only heard on TV from one of the royal family.

"Only the idea of how ironic it is that when you often meet new people, or people enter a room unannounced, their first impression, that first moment in time they witness, is so easily misconstrued."

She lifted an eyebrow but she didn't look pleased. The words had been a gamble, almost a challenge to her not to believe or judge what she'd just seen.

"Am I right in assuming that you're from the organization?" I asked when it was clear no one else was going to say anything.

"I am indeed." She lifted her head and straightened her back, not that it hadn't already looked like she had a poker up her ass. I glanced at Minsheng, who gave me an apologetic shrug.

Before anyone else could speak, Zephyr returned. He padded to my side and then sat beside me. I instinctively reached out to rest my hand on him.

"Well, let me introduce you. This is Zephyr, the dragon I've bonded with."

"I'm Iris," she eventually replied. "From the organization."

"Hello, Iris," Zephyr replied. She jumped, and this time I couldn't help but grin. She clearly hadn't been expecting him to talk.

"I'd like to take this opportunity to say thank you." I decided to take over the conversation and steer it where I wanted. "When Minsheng found us and offered us a home, it saved us from a very difficult situation. And the training and wisdom he has supplied since have been invaluable. I couldn't have asked for a better Shishou or friend."

"That is a big part of what the organization exists for." Iris stepped forward. "We have protected mythicals and put in place a network of Shishous to train and guide bonded elves. It has been many years since we have been privileged to have an elf under our care, but we take our responsibility very seriously."

I nodded, having expected something like this from Minsheng's description. I had a feeling they were going to want to give their little speech about how important the organization was before we could get to anything else of importance.

"It is clear that the organization's wishes and your own have not entirely matched, but in light of all the recent events and the request for further funding that Minsheng has put to us, we decided to come and see for ourselves how your dojo is being run and where you are placed with your abilities and the other mythicals now with you."

"Wonderful," I replied. "As you can see, this is the area we've been forced to expand into. Currently we have makeshift rooms up here and a small roof garden."

She looked over it from where she stood. I didn't want to draw attention to anything in particular.

"And you wish to build more permanent bedrooms and move the roof garden above those? Is that correct?"

"Yes."

"Is the roof garden essential? I mean, as much as it's nice to be able to sit in the sun in LA, I've been led to understand that you were shot at up here a couple of hours ago."

"I was, yes," I replied. "You walked in on my finishing up business with the sniper who attempted it."

"And Zephyr saved you? That sounds very lucky to me."

"I've been working on a personal barrier technique using my abilities," I found myself saying before I could keep the words from coming out. "I slowed the bullet, giving Zephyr time to get in the way."

"Your ability to alter the trajectory of projectiles has been documented. The file notes I was given made no mention of you being able to slow them when they were close to you." She scribbled on the clipboard and I frowned.

These people need to watch our fights too, Zephyr said before yawning. *They're so misinformed without us.*

Tell me about it. Would save us a lot of effort.

"Anyway, as fascinating as that is, it doesn't preclude my point. I don't feel a garden is necessary, nor a small beach and toys," she continued, pointing at the sand and deck chairs to one side.

"Oh, the sand is there for the fire salamanders," I replied. "It's essential to their wellbeing. They use it for recharging at the end of each day. The sand soaks up the heat from the sun, and at sunset, they come up here and settle into it. If we didn't have that, they'd need to go to the beach each day. As today's sniper incident proved, that's hardly safe for them."

She blinked and looked at Minsheng as if she didn't believe what I was saying.

"Perhaps we can show you later. It's quite spectacular to see them light up and change colors as they do so," Minsheng replied, smiling. I'd never heard him sound so serious. I wasn't the only one who felt the pressure of this visit.

"That does sound like something I should be aware of and record. You're the first Shishou to have fire salamanders under your care."

"Well, they're more under Aella, Daisy, and Erlan's care, really. One of them bonded with Erlan, and the rest are looked after by Daisy and Aella."

"Your sister has basic veterinary qualifications, I understand," Iris said as she turned back to the opening to the bedrooms and the route back into the building. I moved closer, hoping she'd get the hint and go inside. I'd had enough of being out in the open and exposed.

So much so that it took me a moment to process what

she'd said about Daisy, especially after Minsheng answered in the affirmative.

Thankfully, he took it upon himself to step in and give Iris a tour of the building. I settled in behind with Zephyr.

The painful twist in my stomach was still there, and I was more than a little worried. This hadn't been a good start to an assessment of us and whether we were worthy of funding.

I could only hope the next few minutes improved her impression of us and the building's purpose and usefulness.

CHAPTER TWELVE

"Well, there are a lot of different things packed in here," Iris said after Minsheng finished the tour. I smiled, grateful for that compliment. She'd asked a lot of questions and scrawled many more notes through the course of the last hour.

On top of that, the cops had arrived and taken away our sniper, and I'd been given little choice but to make a statement. It helped that some of the situation had been caught on live TV, but if anything, that only made them more insistent on having the facts straight.

Iris had calmly stayed in the background while I'd been dealing with the law enforcement, as if she didn't want to be noticed if she could help it.

As soon as they were gone, she'd insisted on continuing, however, not even waiting for us to catch our breath. Minsheng seemed to expect this and took over again, but I felt as compelled as he did to explain when she asked questions about the dojo.

"Please explain again the relationship you have with the

human. Lyra, is it?" I nodded. "You say she runs a dojo here."

"Yes. While I was at the Sanctuary, she kept the warehouse safe for us, cleaned it up, and refitted it to be a dojo and a source of income in and of itself. Many now come to train here because they believe they're learning from the best."

"The best?" she asked, raising that irritating eyebrow again. "That's a bold claim."

"It's what they believe. I don't claim anything so grand, but I do help Lyra teach them and appreciate the financial boost it provides. Especially since I understand the organization felt Erlan and I didn't need any financial support despite the intensive training we do. Running a dojo allows me to both train and earn."

Iris frowned and stared at me for a moment. I had a feeling I'd directly challenged an opinion she held, but I was starting not to care. She was being extremely difficult to deal with, and the scrutiny was unhelpful at best.

"I can see why, with this many mouths to feed and the supplies and materials you must all get through, things are financially tight. It's also clear that you feel your friend has earned her right to use the building as her own dojo—"

"*Our* dojo," I replied, cutting her off. "I teach and earn money from it too. She's not just using it for her own gain. She's even paying rent."

"Right." Iris' frown deepened, more lines appearing on her face. "I think the space could perhaps be better used. The whole floor where you used to sleep when you were first living here is now a changing area and recreation room. That could easily be several bedrooms. And—"

"They are bedrooms at night. There are so many people staying here for safety now that we still need further bedrooms above."

"Perhaps we should introduce you to everyone who lives here over dinner later," Minsheng said. "Quite a few are out at the moment, and the dojo will open for its first lesson shortly. I understand you wanted to see some of our training and Aella's and Zephyr's current skill level?"

I blinked, the only outside reflection that I wasn't sure I liked this new direction.

Yay, we get to be performing monkeys, Zephyr boomed in my head. I could imagine the eye roll that went with it, although I didn't dare look his way. I felt similar. If it got us funding, I could show off with him for a bit, however.

"That would be perfect," Iris replied, the first sign of enthusiasm she'd given. Was this why she was here? To put us through our paces and see what we could really do?

If that was what she wanted to see, we could do that.

Minsheng got started, guiding the pair of us through the usual training sessions, starting with flying together, going through combat situations, and then finally the control of my abilities. We demonstrated how I used them to help us work together, and then the newest trick we were capable of: me controlling Zephyr's breath weapon.

By the time we were done, both Zephyr and I were exhausted, but we'd gained an audience. Ronan and Daisy were both nearby.

Ronan came over to Minsheng and Iris and very politely bowed. He then introduced himself.

"Daisy has informed me that you're from the organization and have been supporting this building and our care here. You have my gratitude and respect, madam."

This made Iris blush, and I caught her glancing at Ronan's strong and very well-defined muscles a couple of times. She wasn't unaffected by what she saw, after all. The whole time Zephyr and I had been going through our capabilities, she had stood with the same slight frown on her face, making notes.

Not even moving gas clouds or our flying had impressed her.

Before anyone else could speak, Ronan slipped into a trance.

"What's going on?" Iris demanded. I explained as quickly as I could, more than a little concerned. The last time this had happened, Ronan had been given bad news about the Sanctuary and the orbs that led mythicals to it. Could something else have happened?

"It's best to give him some space and hope it won't be long," Minsheng said. "Let us go somewhere more comfortable, and you can see the plans we've drawn up for our proposed expansion. I'm sure you'll have questions."

Before Iris could do more than nod, however, Ronan snapped back to us.

His eyes were wide, and he clenched his jaw and growled.

"The Sanctuary needs me," he said, looking straight to me. "Aella, I humbly request for you to release me from your service here so I may return to aid them."

"Of course," I replied. "But what's wrong?"

"There's little time. I must get back. There has been some kind of attack."

"The orbs again?" I asked as I hurried toward the stairs with him.

"I believe it is possible, but my information is limited."

"I'll drive you back. It will be quicker," Daisy said, going to the stash of keys we kept in a small cabinet.

"Thank you. I would appreciate the aid in such a swift form of travel." Ronan nodded and bowed to me before the pair rushed off.

"Guess that means I'm making dinner this evening," Minsheng replied. "I'll get Chris to man reception when the dojo opens."

"No, I'll do it. Chris understands the plans best and can aid Iris in understanding what we wish to do here."

It looked like both Minsheng and Iris might object to that idea, but I didn't stick around to hear either voice that opinion.

I wanted time alone with Zephyr and time to think, and the only way I was going to get that was at the front desk while everyone else was busy.

You're worried about Ronan and the Sanctuary, Zephyr said as he joined me, curling up in the reception area and taking up most of it.

Yes. And about Jacobs and if he's after us. We're not getting anywhere so far.

We're doing what we can. That's all you can do until we know more.

I reached out for Zephyr and ran a hand down his neck. His words helped, but until I knew what had happened, I wouldn't be able to relax.

For the next few minutes, I had the welcome distraction of letting people in for the first lesson. A few seemed sad to see me on reception and to learn that was where I'd be staying while they were taught by Lyra, but they soon accepted it.

Needs must. I could have asked Erlan, but he'd been grilled by Iris once already and had gone to hide. Until sunset, we were going to show Iris what the fire salamanders were capable of. I didn't want to bother him again until then.

He wasn't used to the human world of politics and conditions. Everything he'd needed at the Sanctuary had been there for him, and his personal space and right to his opinion had been respected.

I'd also considered Holfin, but he was starting dinner while Chris was occupied and had since been sent to the store for the supplies we needed. There was no one else to take reception, and it gave me time to think.

Not that I got much further with my thoughts. We needed more information, as Zephyr had said.

The second lesson was well underway when I heard a commotion outside and what sounded like Holfin's raised voice.

I ran to the door and flung it open, feeling rather than seeing Zephyr follow.

"Aella, come quickly. Some mythicals are being attacked!" Holfin hurried toward the building until he spotted me.

"Where?" I asked as Zephyr launched into the air, flying up and over me and buffeting me with the air from the powerful downbeat of his wings.

"Three blocks that way. By the store. They were trying to come here. I bumped into them while paying for our groceries. They asked how to get here, but some people were lingering outside and challenged them. It was all I could do to run back here and get you."

By the time he finished speaking, I'd reached him.

"It's okay. Get inside and find Minsheng. Tell him we've got incoming and that I'll be back with them as soon as I can."

The instructions broke through the dwarf's panic, and he sprinted in as fast as his short legs could carry him.

Without wasting a second, I pushed myself into the air and powered after Zephyr.

I see them, Zephyr said a moment later. He was flying ahead of me and above the level of the buildings.

I rose to join him and we moved together, with me slotting into the familiar position on his back as he propelled us closer to the danger.

It wasn't long before I could see what Holfin had been talking about.

There were three people, clearly mythicals by their gnome-like faces. One had a strange furry creature with a small set of wings sprouting out of its back with him as well. They were being attacked by a group of five young men wielding baseball bats, hockey sticks, and other makeshift weapons.

One of the gnomes was fighting back, aided by his furry companion, but the other two were clearly being beaten.

"Half-breed scum. You don't belong here," one of the young men yelled before spitting on a prone gnome.

"Stop that right now," I bellowed as loudly as I could, getting the attention of a couple of the attackers. Zephyr roared a moment later, the sound so overpowering everyone stopped and stared.

"Leave these people alone," I added as Zephyr landed a few feet away and I half-leaped, half-slid off his back. I hurried forward but the nearest attacker either took this for a threat or he wasn't scared of Zephyr because he swung a hockey stick at me. I hit him with a blast of air before he could reach me and knocked him off his feet. He crashed into another man and they both went down.

"I don't know what has made you decide to hate these people so much just for looking different, but you won't touch another hair on their heads, or so help me God, I will teach you all a lesson." Anger poured from every fiber of my body at the abuse they were dishing out, and I knew I shook from head to toe.

It looked like the nearest might argue with me or try to put up a fight, but one of the others put a hand on his arm and pulled him back.

"You're her, aren't you? The bitch who started all this?"

"If you mean that I'm the half-elf who spent months of her life being hunted by a secret government agency just because I was born and wouldn't let them kill the dragon I found, then yes, I'm her." I didn't look at them as I spoke, instead going to the two injured gnomes. One was barely conscious, moaning in pain but otherwise unresponsive. The other managed to sit up, and the third came to my side.

"We're not going to let you ruin our world and start wars." One of the men came closer, putting his bat down by his feet where I could easily see it while I crouched.

I stood again.

"I don't plan on ruining this world *or* starting wars, and neither does any other mythical race or creature I know. We just want to live, work, enjoy life, and not get beaten up by people who believe a bunch of lies and rumors about us. I don't know what you've been told, but we've been on this planet for millennia. So far, the human race has done just fine. Us not hiding in the shadows anymore doesn't change anything, does it?"

The guy still looked angry, but he didn't speak.

"Now, if you'll excuse me, I'm going to take these poor men you've hurt to get medical treatment. You ever want to talk about what you've done or learn about mythicals and what we're actually like and want in life, you can come to my dojo and ask me. It's three blocks that way."

I turned my back on the men, knowing Zephyr would keep an eye on them, and used my powers to lift the unconscious gnome as gently as I could.

"Can you walk?" I asked the one sitting. He nodded, and his friend put an arm around his shoulders and helped him to his feet.

"We were coming to find you. A dwarf in the store said you had offered him a home when humans had threatened him," the least injured said, although he sported a split lip and a black eye.

"Yeah, he came to get me and Zephyr here. You'll be safe at my place," I replied, having no idea where we'd accommodate them or how long they'd need to stay. One thing was for sure; they were going to need medical treatment.

While the thugs gaped at what I could do, I used my abilities to help all three injured gnomes to my dojo, with

Zephyr flying above us and circling to keep us safe. I looked back a couple of times and noticed the thugs were following at a distance. They could watch if they needed or wanted to. It didn't change anything.

Minsheng, Iris, and Chris were standing by the door with Holfin when I got back. They rushed forward to help the rescued gnomes. Chris ran off to get an airbed, and we tucked it out of the way down the corridor that led nowhere so the poor gnome could rest. Minsheng then fetched the first aid kit, and Iris transformed into the most matronly nurse possible.

It was clear she had experience with injuries because she didn't flinch at the sight of the hurt gnomes and immediately started tending the nastiest-looking wounds.

"His injuries should be seen by a medical expert. If you call an ambulance, I will go with him to the hospital and cover any medical costs from the organization's expense account," she said. "They'll understand."

"Thank you," I said a fraction of a second before the least hurt gnome did.

As Chris picked up his phone and started dialing, she moved on to the one who was limping, quickly diagnosed a sprain, and cleaned several cuts. Finally she checked out the least injured, although the furball that had come with him had to be placated first.

"It's all right, Katrina. She's helping," he said, stroking the creature with one hand.

"Do you mind me asking what she is?" I said as I handed him and his friend some painkillers.

"She's a sphinx. At least, I think that's what she is. She has the body of a cat, wings like an eagle, and she joined us from seemingly nowhere while we were telling riddles in the middle of the desert."

"Nice! She's beautiful and as welcome here as you are. We've already got a few fire salamanders, a centaur who's been called elsewhere for now, and you've met one of the dwarves."

"I'm Justin. This is Tristan, and our very hurt friend is Grim. I can't thank you enough for stepping in when you did. We were hopelessly..." His voice trailed off, and he looked like he might cry.

"It's okay," I said. "The worst is over now. Rest, get your strength back, and worry about nothing. I'm sure Grim will recover, and you'll all be able to look back on this as an unpleasant episode before a much brighter new chapter."

I rested a hand on his shoulder before Iris and Minsheng beckoned me to a huddle by the reception desk. Zephyr came too.

"I will conclude my inspection of your facility here and its use," Iris said, "and I will go with this poor injured gnome to ensure no one else harms him or takes advantage."

I nodded in response, sure she was very capable of the latter.

"My scruples insist I confess that I was going to recommend the dojo element be shut down here and a smaller addition be made to the building, but the last half-hour has changed my mind. Your building has become a beacon for mythicals of every kind, and they clearly believe in your strength and ability to protect them."

"Thank you," I replied, exhaling with relief.

"Yes, well, you are definitely capable, and your mentor

insists you get stronger every day. I don't doubt more will come here seeking your protection, and you must have the space for them. I will authorize the additional building on the condition it becomes a sanctuary. I assume this is acceptable to you?"

"Of course." I wasn't going to argue, although I suspected I had just been used as a pawn in settling some rivalry. The organization had never known where the Sanctuary was, and Minsheng had made it clear they were surprised by how many mythicals were living there. Far more than they'd predicted would be. Far more than we'd hoped.

When the ambulance arrived, Iris went back to nurse mode, and she and Grim were whisked away.

I sank into the nearest sofa and almost cried. Today had been full of so many different threats and difficulties that I wasn't sure I could lift my arms anymore. When Zephyr sat down and rested his head in my lap, I sighed. At least I was never alone in this mess.

CHAPTER THIRTEEN

"Daisy's back," Minsheng said from the top of the stairs as I sparred with Lyra for one of our classes to see.

"I'll leave you in Lyra's capable hands," I said. "I've got someone I urgently need to catch up with."

There were a few sad groans, but most of the class let me leave without a problem. I hurried up the stairs, Zephyr beating me into the room above, and we met Daisy in the kitchen.

She was sitting at the table looking tired, a hot cup of coffee in her hands. I went to her and gave her a hug.

"You must have driven pretty much nonstop," I said as I sat down at the table.

"Feels like it, but I did make sure I was safe and had enough sleep. Ronan was really eager to get there, though. And once I heard what had happened, I knew I needed to come back."

"Tell me everything, and then we'll tell you about our excitement," I replied.

"I can go one better. Ronan gave me this. He asked you to be very careful with it and keep it safe. I'm not sure Lorcan approved of him giving it to you either."

I opened my mouth to ask what it was, but Daisy placed it in my hands. It was a smooth white stone, but the object was warm, not chilly as I'd expected it to be.

As I held it, it began to glow. Only a little at first, but it grew brighter over a few seconds until it lit up my palm. A warm orange light emanated from it.

"Cool. He said you could tell if you could use it if it lit up. Guess that's what he meant."

"What does it do?"

"It connects your mind with Ronan's. Sort of how he connects with Lorcan, but the stone lets Ronan and anyone who can power it connect."

"Which is why he asked me to keep it safe."

"Yes. He was very concerned that you understood how important it was and how centaurs don't give these out lightly," Daisy said before sipping her drink. "Apparently, Lorcan's biggest objection was that I was bringing it to you, and it wasn't being handed to you directly. When I couldn't activate it, he grew less grumpy, but only a little."

I grinned, able to imagine what Daisy meant.

"He said when you were ready to converse with him to just find somewhere you could rest and press it to your forehead. It does the rest."

"So, I'm going to do that trance thing Ronan did?" I asked to clarify.

"That's what he implied."

"All right. Thank you, Daisy," I said as I got to my feet. "I'm going to be in my room for a bit. Probably best no one disturbs me for a while unless it's an emergency. I'll come back once I'm done."

Zephyr and I went up to the roof and into the small area where we slept. I settled on the bed, leaning against the wall, and concentrated on the stone again. The light had faded as I'd moved, but I only had to look at the stone for it to come back.

All right, here goes, I sent to Zephyr and touched it to my head.

Almost immediately, I was sucked into absolute darkness. A moment later, I was standing in a room. I couldn't see the walls, but I felt like they were there. Zephyr stepped up to my left, his warm presence familiar.

Looks like I get to come along for this ride, he said, his voice still in my head. It was strange, but given our bond, I guessed anything in my head would involve him too.

A moment later, a small light window appeared. It grew bigger, making me squint, and then Ronan stepped through it. With a snap, it shut, leaving the three of us somehow perfectly illuminated in the pitch-black space.

"Daisy delivered the seeing stone, then. Good. Lorcan will be relieved to know my instinct was correct," Ronan said.

"Yes. Please, let Lorcan know that we will keep it safe," I replied.

Ronan gave me a small bow before looking at Zephyr. "I had wondered if your bond would enable you both to be here, but this is the first time it has been demonstrated. The bond between the two of you must be very strong indeed."

I reached for Zephyr as Ronan spoke, and the dragon

leaned into me. The affection between us was clear, and it made Ronan dip his chin again.

No one needed to speak. We'd made our true feelings for each other clear, something we'd not done in front of any of the others. This space felt safe, and I had a feeling Ronan understood better than the others could.

"As much as I would love to talk to you about how this works and why I can talk to you from so far away, I understand something is up and you wished for this conversation to happen urgently. Please, Ronan, tell me what's happened, and I'll help as best I can."

He sighed, a long exhale that spoke of his sadness.

"I believe the agents have returned. They have been seen many times around the Sanctuary's borders. At first the council insisted we do as always and turn these people away, encouraging them far from our borders, but they are a lot more resistant to the natural magic here, and several got through the barrier that protects the Sanctuary."

"Oh, no. Is anyone hurt?"

"Only minor injuries. But I opted to capture the agents. If we let them go, they could lead more to us. However, I cannot get them to tell me anything, and the council wishes me to kill them. I had hoped for you to propose an alternative."

"I could…possibly. But I gained no information from the sniper who tried to kill me. It sounds like your captives might be less than cooperative."

"That is possible, but I will not kill those who could be turned over to authorities in your own world or detained in another manner. And I would learn all I could first. I do not understand the politics of the human world, but I believe the actions of the agency to now be against the law."

"I understand. I can't say if the agency is still officially running in secret, but the American people would want to know about it."

"Will you come, then?"

"I'll come. I have questions of my own. Someone needs to give me answers."

Ronan bowed again, and I did the same, Zephyr following suit. A moment later, Ronan turned and left the area, and my eyes opened back in our small room, Zephyr beside me.

That was strange, he said as we looked at each other.

I can imagine. You just sort of came along for the ride.

Something like that. I think I could have resisted it, but it was easier to join you, and I wanted to hear it too.

I'd have filled you in.

I know, but let's just say it explains a memory or two. I think Tuviel and Azargad once had a conversation like that too, only there was an entire army of centaurs in theirs.

Sounds intense, I replied, leaning into him, giving him a moment.

It's not very clear, and any emotions once associated with the memory are long gone. We should focus on the matter at hand.

I nodded. *We've got to try to find the quickest way to get to the Sanctuary. But I can't ask Daisy to drive us again so soon, and everyone else is needed here.*

We could fly. Our eyes met again at his suggestion.

It would be tiring.

For you, more so. You'd need to use your abilities to keep the wind from blowing you off my back and keep the forces down.

I sighed. He was right, and it was the best way. At worst, we'd have to find somewhere to rest along the route, but at best, it left everyone else here to keep the warehouse safe and run the dojo.

Despite the plan, I couldn't help but worry about everyone I was leaving behind. It seemed every few days I was needed to defend mythicals who were looking at the warehouse as a refuge, just as I had many months ago. I couldn't be in two places at once.

I'd promised Ronan I'd go to the Sanctuary, however, and I needed answers. For now, it was my best course of action. I needed to stop reacting to the things the agency did and start making proper plans of my own. This was a way I could begin to do that.

I packed up my bag, putting the seeing stone safely in the bottom and anything else I thought I might need on top of it.

For some reason, my eyes fixed on the pot I'd been given by the water master at the Sanctuary. It had a sprout-ling in it. Although it had been for me to test my abilities, not grow the seed the normal way, I was pleased it was alive. I opted to bring it as well.

Once it was safely in the top of the pack with a cup over it so it wouldn't get crushed, I made my way down to the main section of the warehouse to find Minsheng.

He was in the kitchen with Daisy, the two of them talking.

"Thought you'd be heading out," Minsheng said, his eyes flicking to the pack I carried. "I can drive the bus if you want."

I shook my head, smiling at his name for the armored vehicle Ronan's friend had acquired for us the first time we'd been to the Sanctuary.

"We're going to fly," I replied. "We need you here. I need to know the dojo and all the mythicals here are being looked after by someone with experience and respect, and Erlan needs you to keep training him. This war is clearly not over."

"Daisy was telling me what she knew. Sounds like Jacobs is trying to take out the Sanctuary while the world is focused on us."

"And he's smearing us in the media at every turn too," Chris added as he came into the kitchen, making it clear he'd heard plenty of the conversation already. "They let the sniper go. He was just found dead, and they made it look like Zephyr did it."

Shitsticks.

I didn't do it.

I know, I replied, reaching a hand out to him.

"Are they looking to charge us with it?" I asked a moment later.

"I doubt they'll have enough evidence, or they would have already. But the media are putting it out everywhere." Chris looked sad. "I'm going to see if we can prove you couldn't have been there. We can essentially publish your alibi or something. Try not to worry about it."

"I'll see what that lawyer can help us with to stop this kind of thing too," Minsheng added.

I looked at them for a moment, grateful for this small

group of people who'd been by my side for the best part of a year now.

"Hold the fort for me. Take in any mythicals who come to us, and keep working on the building expansion," I said to finish. "I'll be back as soon as I have answers and the Sanctuary is safe enough they no longer need me."

Daisy hugged me before going to give Zephyr a rub behind the ears, and Chris nodded and grinned.

When Minsheng came to give me a goodbye hug, he leaned in close to my ear.

"Try to get the Sanctuary to move closer. I know you'll want to protect them and us. Don't let the council dig their heels in just because they wish they could still hide in legends and stories."

I nodded, grateful for his words.

A moment later, Chris handed me a box of granola bars.

"You're going to need these," he said. Laughter filled the room as we stuffed as many of them into my pack as we could. I was as ready as I was going to get.

"All right," I said. "Ronan is waiting for me, and I've got some agents to go give merry hell to."

I smiled and hurried away before I started to cry. It felt like I was going off to war without them, and that was something I'd never done before. I suspected I was going to feel just as divided when I left the Sanctuary to come back again. I had friends in both places, and both places were in danger.

We'll help both be safe, Zephyr said, once again making it clear he could either hear my thoughts or feel my conflicted emotions.

We've got to get there first, I replied as we made our way back up to the roof.

On the way, Erlan appeared.

"You're heading out again, aren't you?" he asked, his green eyes extra-wide. I studied his elven features and noted how young he still looked. I didn't know how old he was, just that this human place was still new to him and he'd lived in safety for so long. Had I doomed him?

"The Sanctuary needs my help," I replied.

"I know. We all do, and I'll keep doing what I can here. But promise me one thing, Aella."

"What?" I asked, surprised by his fierce look and the light in his eyes.

"Promise me you won't blame yourself for what's happening. We'd have eventually been in a war anyway. The human population was growing. The agency was getting stronger. You've given us hope in a war that was inevitable, even if you did make it happen sooner."

Erlan hugged me at the same time as I did him.

"I'll keep training with Minsheng and do what I can to protect this place until you return. Don't worry about us," he said as we pulled back.

"You know I'll worry about you anyway, right?"

"Yeah, of course, but you should worry less. You've laid a good foundation here, and your friends are well-prepared."

I nodded, and we grinned. Sometimes the right person saying the right thing could make a situation a lot better. The nagging feeling that something far bigger than we'd ever faced was coming didn't go away, but at least the people Zephyr and I were leaving behind were experienced against the agents. And the defending team kept getting larger and stronger.

Trying to push all the worries aside, I hurried back to Zephyr's side and out onto the roof. It was still fairly light out, but there wasn't much daylight left. We were going to be flying through the night.

Ready? Zephyr asked.

I responded by jetting into the air, my pack on my back and my eyes on the sky ahead. Zephyr was soon under me and then supporting my weight. I reached for more air, forming it into a streamlined shield around my body that helped us fly.

Feeling pretty good, I then extended it around Zephyr too, to help him get up to speed and keeping him from getting as tired. After all, he had to do most of the work. I just had to hold on and keep myself from getting too drained.

Traveling east at the speed Zephyr could reach soon had the sun setting behind us and the night air growing colder. I was glad I'd thought to wear warm clothing and that my slipstream of solid air kept the wind from being too cold on my exposed skin.

A couple of hours it was clear I couldn't keep it up, however. I slowly eased off areas of the protection I was giving Zephyr, letting him know as I did.

I can keep flying for a while, he replied. *Let me know when you want a break.*

Not yet. The Sanctuary needs us.

Don't worry. We'll get there far faster than the bus could. But you need to have some energy left to help.

I know, but the agents are often attacking at night. And it's night.

They've held the fort so far.

True.

I sighed and tried to focus on something else, which wasn't as hard as I thought since the stars came out and the world transformed beneath us. Nighttime with the stars and the moon always made me feel calmer.

CHAPTER FOURTEEN

As the night wore on, I grew more tired. I'd already had a full day of using my abilities and training. Before long, we had to take our first break to get some dinner, stopping at a small-town diner. The locals looked wide-eyed at Zephyr, but relaxed when I assured them he was friendly and ordered a massive amount of meat for him.

Of course, he didn't fit into the diner, so we found a patch of grass not far from the building to sit and eat. The waitress was bold enough to give him a stroke. Zephyr even talked to her a little.

Although we'd drawn an audience and it would have been a good PR opportunity, we didn't have time. Our next stop had been somewhere quieter, and I'd taken a power nap, being by far the more exhausted of the two of us.

After some snacks and drinks, we got in the air for the third time. We'd been flying for a couple of hours and I was considering asking Zephyr for one final break when I noticed lights ahead. I assumed we were coming up to a small town but as it came into view, it looked like some kind of office park or office-based military installation.

It wasn't quiet either, having several cars in the parking lot and lights on in a couple of the buildings. It didn't take us long to fly over it, but it made me wonder where we were.

Only another half an hour or so and I think we'll be there, Zephyr said. He was starting to sound tired, and I couldn't blame him. We'd flown several hundred miles, possibly even a thousand, in one night. I didn't know exactly where the Sanctuary was, but I was grateful that Zephyr had a good sense of direction.

Despite being tired, I decided to hang on and let Zephyr get us the rest of the way. It was always more effort to land and then get back into the air and up to speed again.

We were still a little way out, but I could see something in the distance that looked like it might be the Sanctuary when I noticed the outline of people up ahead, carrying something that shone.

Is that a group with an orb? I asked Zephyr, knowing his eyesight was better than mine.

It looks like it. I'll slow so we can sneak up on them.

They might be friendly, I pointed out.

They might. And if they are, we can land and escort them the rest of the way. If not...

We'll want the element of surprise.

Exactly.

Zephyr slowed, moving his wings more gently to keep us from making as much noise, and came down lower. Thankfully the moon was ahead of us, so our shadow was behind us. I tried to focus on the people, but it was hard to tell if they were friend or foe.

We need to listen in on what they're saying. Can you create a funnel of air that comes gently from them to us? Zephyr asked.

I lifted my eyebrows at the idea, but I knew to trust Zephyr's suggestions. They were usually based on memories our activities had triggered.

Thinking about what a funnel looked like, I reached out to control the air ahead of us as Zephyr dropped even lower, his wings barely above the ground on each downward stroke.

At first it seemed like nothing had happened, but eventually, they spoke.

"We should be careful. I think we're getting close, and this isn't far from where Rich and his men disappeared last night. The boss said if we found them, we'd find the jackpot," someone said with a Southern twang.

I frowned. This sounded like agents trying to find the Sanctuary.

"I still don't get why we're doing this. Seems like poking a hornet's nest, trying to find this Sanctuary place. If they're as powerful as that girl with the dragon, shouldn't we be leaving them alone?"

"You really want terrorists like that running around in our country doing what they like, Mickey?"

"No, course not, but they can't all be evil. It's like saying all Germans are Nazis and all Native Americans should be shot."

"Sure, but someone's got to work out who is who and which ones are the Nazis or need arresting. I'd rather it was our guys than theirs. And besides, this isn't like you,

Mickey. The boss said when you get close to the Sanctuary, it starts messing with your head. That's all that's happening. It's trying to get us to go in a different direction. We can't let it."

I'd heard enough. These were clearly agents, and I couldn't let them get any closer to the Sanctuary.

Zephyr, I said in my head. *How about we gas this lot and take their orb? Should knock them out till morning.*

As he'd grown, so had the potency of the gas he breathed, and while we hadn't tested it lately, it had knocked the agents out of commission for a couple of hours the last time we'd used it.

Gladly, he replied, and I felt him shift to get the right angle and move forward. He had to make more noise, but I did my best to cover it and keep them oblivious. We were almost above them when they finally noticed they weren't alone.

"What the..." one of them had time to say before Zephyr was above them, breathing gas downward.

Most of them were caught in the initial burst of paralyzing gas and sagged to the ground, neutralized. The two who had been farthest ahead ran.

"Oh, gawd, there's another dragon. They've got another dragon," Mickey yelled, trying to sprint away and stumbling.

"No," I yelled. "It's *that* girl with a dragon, and she doesn't appreciate you threatening innocent creatures out of fear and misguided loyalty to controlling sociopaths."

Zephyr flew on over their heads. One of them drew a gun, but I used my powers to both yank it out of his hands and grab the cloud of gas Zephyr had already created. I pulled the vapor toward them as Zephyr circled and landed, cutting off their path toward the Sanctuary.

They skidded to a halt, glaring at us.

"Tell your boss the Sanctuary is under my protection," I added before I enveloped them in more gas. Mickey tried to run, but he didn't get far. Within another few seconds, the agents were all out cold.

I wafted the dangerous gas away and went to pick up the orb while Zephyr kept an eye on our perimeter and made sure no agents were going to sneak up on us. It had rolled out of the lead agent's hands as he'd gone down, and I stowed it in my pack.

We should move them away from the Sanctuary, I told Zephyr a moment later. *Make sure they can't stumble into it when they come around.*

As I spoke, I lifted the three nearest men with my abilities and floated them away from us. I followed at a distance, not wanting to create any tracks for them to follow but trampling theirs.

Zephyr grabbed a couple in his claws and flew up with them. We placed them on the other side of a bunch of bushes, ensuring they'd be in shade when the sun first came up. We were in a desert-like area, and I wasn't cruel.

By the time they were all out of the way, I was exhausted. The sky was just beginning to brighten on the eastern horizon, and the Sanctuary couldn't have looked more inviting.

Zephyr sensed my tiredness because he flew over to me and crouched so I could climb onto his back and let him lift me up and away from the agents.

Although he still had the energy to fly, I noticed he

didn't rush. We floated and glided where possible, and his long and powerful wingspan worked almost effortlessly to keep us up when the natural air currents didn't.

We were in the Sanctuary before I spotted the familiar face of Ronan. He was clearly guarding a section of the perimeter to our left. Zephyr banked that way as I waved.

"I must confess, I didn't expect to see you so soon. Did you fly the whole way?" Ronan asked by way of a greeting.

"Yes," Zephyr replied as I slid off his back.

I told Ronan what we'd encountered on the way and how we'd flown through the night, ending up by informing him about the group of eight agents we'd prevented from getting any closer.

"Thank you," Ronan said. "We've had a busy night. Agents seem to be trying to find us from many directions, and it's clear they're narrowing our location down."

"I'd say the same thing based on the conversations we overheard. We should talk to the agents you have captured and the council as soon as possible."

"Yes, they asked to see you when they heard you were coming, but I think they'd understand if you rested first. After all, they're not expecting you yet."

I considered objecting to the idea and getting straight to business, but the Sanctuary was no longer threatened, and the agents they held were unlikely to go anywhere. There was time to rest.

Ronan led us toward an incredibly familiar log cabin on the perimeter. I almost laughed.

I'd have marveled at how something like this was possible as we went inside, but I knew there were several earth elves in the Sanctuary, and for them, this must have been fairly easy. I did notice that the doorway on the balcony was far larger than it used to be. Big enough for an almost fully grown dragon.

"The earth master likes to stay out here sometimes," Ronan said, confirming my suspicions. "The city center can get a bit busy and that makes it hard to think. Especially now that there's extras coming in."

"Are they making it here okay?"

"Some. We suspect some are giving up, but if many more arrive, we'll need to expand."

"We're expanding the warehouse, too," I replied.

"You have received funding from your superiors?"

"I wouldn't call them superiors," I said as I headed toward the stairs, Zephyr momentarily outside. "But the people who pay the bills, yeah."

Ronan chuckled as he went into his room. I continued to climb and reached the small landing at the top. Only two doors led off it rather than the three in the previous two designs of the cabin, and I took the one toward the front of the cabin, opening it to find Zephyr waiting for me on the balcony. I let him in and marveled at the view.

The Sanctuary sat in front of us, the city a thing of beauty. How could anyone want to destroy the gifts that could make something so stunning?

They don't understand, Zephyr said. *And some people don't want to. It's easier to hate what challenges you than to change and learn.*

True, but we need some sleep. Just let's make sure we thank the earth master when we get into the city. He made a room big enough for both of us.

I wouldn't be surprised if Ronan also had something to do

with it, Zephyr replied as we made our way toward the space in the middle. It was an oval bed, larger than any humanoid needed, and on it were pillows and blankets. In short, whoever had made it knew Zephyr and I slept side by side and one of us needed a lot of space.

Despite how tired I was, I struggled to fall asleep. Everything that had happened in one day was too much for my tired brain to forget about.

On top of that, part of me was proud of how far we'd come. There'd been a time I had tried to defend my warehouse while flying around like a drunk, and tonight I'd used the air to help us fly hundreds of miles in a few hours.

When I'd first begun using magic and protecting the baby dragon I'd found, I'd never thought something like this was possible. But I knew I still had a long way to go, and so did Zephyr.

Can't sleep either, he said as I rolled over again.

No. I'm too buzzed and worried.

About everyone we need to protect?

A little. And Crawley's daughter and Jacobs. Something doesn't add up there, and I wouldn't be surprised if the despicable man has taken her.

If so, she could be anywhere.

Maybe, I replied, not convinced.

If someone was getting the orbs activated for the agents to use, could it be Crawley's daughter? Or another mythical, for that matter? Did the agency have other half-breeds among their ranks? After all, Knox had been one.

I couldn't believe a mythical would do it willingly, Knox excluded, but that meant I'd need to find out where they were being held. I'd never done anything sneakily until tonight. Could we even come close to doing something like that?

We don't know we'll need to. I'm sure we'll get answers out of the agents here once we've slept.

Assuming the council will let us try.

They'll let us, Zephyr replied with a dark tone in his voice. He sounded confident, and it made me feel a little better.

Rolling back over, I snuggled against his side and focused on his heartbeat. It was steadier than a human's and a little slower, the perfect background thump to fall asleep to.

CHAPTER FIFTEEN

Hunger woke me, followed by the cold. I arose to see that Zephyr was gone and the main balcony door was ajar. At first I felt disoriented. I almost never woke up after him, but as I tried to reach for him with my mind, I heard voices and realized he was talking to Ronan outside.

For a moment I considered going out to the balcony and flying down, but I could smell the heavenly scent of fried bacon, and my stomach won the battle with another rumble.

I made myself presentable, repacked my small bag, and hurried downstairs. There was a plate of food keeping warm in an oven, so I fished it out and got to work. I'd only taken a few bites when Ronan poked his head through the doorway.

"Zephyr said you were awake, and he clearly knew what he was talking about when he said you'd go for sustenance first." Ronan smiled as he came closer.

"He knows me well, and he can also sense my presence

and the majority of my thoughts and feelings. Our bond gives him an advantage none could match."

Spoilsport, I heard Zephyr say.

It made me grin even more. I quickly ate the food while Ronan gathered the few belongings he wished to take with him and washed a large empty bowl and another plate. I could only assume they'd already eaten and briefly wondered how much Zephyr had packed away.

"To the council, then," I said as we put away the clean crockery. I picked up my bag once more.

I was surprised to see the sun was past its zenith as I stepped outside. Once I had fallen asleep, it hadn't been a short nap.

And you snored, Zephyr said a moment later.

Not as much as you, I replied.

How do you know? You were fast asleep.

Ronan informed me. Apparently, a certain centaur didn't get anywhere near as much sleep as we did.

Do you think he'll forgive us?

Eventually. But probably not until the Sanctuary is safe again.

We'd better get to work then, he replied, his mouth forming the familiar lizard version of a grin. It was infectious and made me feel lighter for a moment. Somehow Zephyr always made me feel better, no matter what we were up against.

The city didn't seem as unwelcoming this time, although it could have been because the sun was shining on it and the elves were milling around. I also didn't see Seth, which helped.

By the time we reached the council building, all but

Lorcan were present, the message we were heading that way having been passed on by someone without us needing to ask.

"Hello again, Aella-Faye," Vestan, the male elf who had always greeted me kindly said. "I understand you turned many agents away from our borders last night. You have my gratitude."

"Don't mention it," I replied. "I'll always be willing to help deter them from coming here. The Sanctuary is a beacon for all mythicals, and I'm continually at its service. Which is why I'm here."

"Of course. As soon as we have Lorcan, we will begin. It's not like him to be late, but I understand many other guards on our borders have information to report, and he doesn't like to come to us until he has all the necessary details."

I bowed to Vestan, understanding but equally being crestfallen at their predicament. Something had to be done. And soon.

Thankfully Lorcan didn't take much longer to arrive. I listened as he briefly informed the council of three other incidents involving agents. All of them had possessed orbs. Two groups had gotten away with theirs.

Reminded of the one I'd taken, I reached into my bag, drew it out, and placed it on the small table near me.

"I can at least return this one to you," I said. "I'm not sure where it came from originally, but it's a start."

"Again, you have our thanks for stopping the agents with this one and for returning it to us. Ronan informed us that you intended to answer his request for aid as quickly as you could. We didn't expect to see you quite so soon, however." Sierrathen sat and placed her hands on the arms of her chair.

This seemed to indicate the start of the council meeting, and not for the first time, I wondered where my seat was. Or Zephyr's. I kept that thought to myself, however. Now wasn't the time for it.

"I flew through the night with Zephyr," I said instead. "It took some air control and a few rest stops, but it meant we were in the perfect place at the right time to stop that group of agents. And send them a little message. No doubt they were very confused when they woke up."

This earned me a chuckle from the dwarf and polite smiles from the others. At least I thought Elowan was smiling. He was some kind of sentient tree, his limbs willow-like. There was something warm and happy about the facial area of his features, but he was droopy in every other respect. A creature of contradictions.

"I'm only sorry we didn't arrive soon enough to help with the other groups." I looked at Lorcan as I said this, meaning every word.

"I appreciate the thought. We managed to handle the rest, thankfully, though I don't doubt they will be back tonight."

"You will have Zephyr and me to patrol again this evening. We'll fly circles around the perimeter all night if we need to."

"Your offer is gladly accepted, and I'm sure will aid us greatly in recovering the other orbs the agents possess." Lorcan bowed in my direction in much the same way Ronan did when he was trying to say thank you for my intentions or words. It was enough. It had been clear on several occasions that when it came to Sanctuary's safety, Lorcan had the final say.

"That is all very well," said Nesryn, the gnome sitting at the opposite end of the table.

I politely gave him my attention, half-expecting him to lead the conversation where I wanted it to go next anyway.

"But we need to come up with a way of stopping the agents getting the orbs in the first place. The last time you were here, you told us you'd dealt with the agency."

"Yes, and officially I have. The human populace believes they have been shut down, but I have a theory about their acquisition of the orbs and how they are activating them. I hope I can stop them from needing the orbs, or at least temporarily delay them and set them back in their plans while I find a way to stop this rogue section."

"Of course you do," Martyl replied, the fairy rolling his eyes and making it clear his words weren't meant as a compliment.

Can I eat him? Zephyr asked in my head, wiping the frown that had appeared there back off as I imagined that.

Probably not. I don't think he'd taste very nice even if you could. Probably better to stick with pizza.

If you insist.

I caught him rolling his eyes and had to fight back a smile. As I got myself under control, I looked at the gnome and fairy, sure they were the two I had to convince.

"An acquaintance with a half-elf daughter came to me a week ago to tell me her daughter was missing. The girl had set off for the Sanctuary, but as we've recently learned by talking to the mythicals here, she hasn't made it. I believe this rogue sector of agents has her captive. It's my intention to rescue her."

"And you believe she's activating the orbs for them?" Vestan asked, sitting forward the tiniest fraction.

"Under duress, yes. And the agents you have captive will be able to aid me in determining how and where she is being held. I'd like to talk to them as soon as possible. If I can find where they're holding this unfortunate mythical, I can rescue her."

"While this seems like a lot of assumptions, I agree that there must be someone with mythical blood helping these agents. I voted to end the lives of the agents so they could endanger us no more, but if you think they can serve some purpose before then, so be it."

"I'd strongly advise against killing the agents," I replied instantly. "The human population won't think kindly of such an action."

"We don't particularly care what the humans think when it's their kind threatening us." Martyr fluttered his wings and glared.

"You should. They're not against you, but they are worried that you won't abide by the morality and rules they've set up to govern their societies. If you do this, they'll become even more frightened, and frightened humans do stupid things."

There was silence after my words, but none of the council members seemed to be moved by what I'd said. I bit down on the angry words I wanted to add. I still needed to help these people, even if they were being stupid. They were probably also scared right now.

"We will make our own minds up on what to do with

our prisoners when the time comes," Sierrathen replied a moment later. "While they are useful to you and will aid in us defending the Sanctuary, we are willing to keep them alive but imprisoned."

"Thank you," I replied. It was a start. "I would like to begin talking to them as soon as possible."

Vestan stood and looked at the female elf beside him, who joined him.

"Ronan can act as your guide and relay to us any answers you obtain, I'm sure."

The centaur bowed to the council as Vestan finished speaking. It was the only warning I was going to get that I had to report what I knew to the council this time.

No doubt they'd want to be part of any decision or plan made in response to that, but while Ronan felt he needed to answer to them, I didn't.

I was the only one in the room with experience of both worlds. And they clearly didn't have a clue about dealing with humans and what would and wouldn't get them the peace they so eagerly wanted.

With no more to say for now, I let Ronan head away and flew outside with Zephyr through the open roof rather than taking the stairs.

"I'm sorry," Ronan said as he led the way down the street. It was quieter than it had been earlier, and I suspected that many of the inhabitants were now settling down to an early evening meal. I'd slept through much of the day, but I made a mental note to pursue the option of food as soon as I'd finished talking to the agents.

Ronan led me to one edge of the Sanctuary and another interesting building. This one was also seemingly made from a single tree, but it didn't have the same smooth bark that grew tall but strong. This was an almost bush-like construction. The branches were much rougher and covered in thorny spikes. It fit in fairly well with the plants that grew in this area of the world naturally.

It had one open side, barely big enough for Zephyr, and on the inside, I saw that branches had been woven into person-sized pods, the walls covered in the same sorts of prickles, and smaller branches forming bars over the pods, equally unfriendly and sharp.

As soon as we entered, I noticed the four agents, each sitting in one of the eight available spaces, gaps between them to make the isolation even more extreme. They all looked my way.

"Wondered if we'd get to see the brat and her oversized pet," one of them said and spat on the floor of his cage. I ignored him, pretty sure he had only acted and spoken this way to get a reaction out of me.

I moved toward the next one in the line.

"I know you work for Jacobs, and I know you've been tasked with getting orbs and finding this place," I said, looking at the others to check I had the attention of all four.

One was trying to look aloof, but I noticed him slow the biting of his nails and tilt his head a fraction to the right so he could hear me a little better.

"I also don't think there would be any prizes for guessing what you intend to do with the inhabitants here, so let me be really clear. It's not happening. Not while I'm here and while my good friend the centaur here is in charge of their defense."

The first spat again and turned his back. I fought back a grin. Getting to one of them was a good enough result right now.

"Finally. I'm pretty sure the young woman turning those orbs on for you has had enough of doing so. Why don't you tell me where she is, and I'll pay her and everyone there a visit."

"Why would we tell you anything?" the agent on my left replied, his chubby frame sporting a few scratches. He clearly hadn't been careful where or how he moved. I took a few steps in his direction and gave him my attention.

"Many reasons. Because you'll die if you don't. The council here has had enough of you and doubts your usefulness. But also because you can't stop me. I could just follow the next set of your friends back to their base, but I'd like to see if you've got enough sense to know that talking gets you an advantage and saves more lives than your own."

The braver agent spoke again. "If they were going to kill us, they'd have done it already."

"No, they were waiting for me to arrive. I had a long way to come. Bit busy in LA, dangling the sniper Jacobs sent to kill me over a pit of pissed-off fire salamanders. And right now, I'm deciding if I want to do the same with you all, or just let Zephyr here fly you out over the Rockies and drop you there."

"You wouldn't," the agent on my right said, getting to his feet.

"Shut up, Merl," Mr. Aloof said, no longer sounding so aloof.

"Oh, Merl, seems you might be the first to see sense.

How about you tell me what you know? We'll see if it matches up with what your sniper friend told me, and then you can have a nice rest somewhere a lot more comfortable. Maybe even a hot meal. Meanwhile I can play a few of my favorite games with these three knuckleheads."

"Don't tell her anything, Merl."

"She already knows a bunch of stuff. It's not like Jacobs has kept it completely secret. And I'm sick and tired of being in a cage I can't move in without being scratched to pieces."

"Jacobs has definitely not kept his secrets very well," I replied, hoping my grin looked more manic than usual. I truly felt smug that he'd already told me something I hadn't known for sure. My bluff was working so far.

"He's got someone turning the orbs on, but we don't know where. We take the orbs to our direct boss when we find them, and they come back to us fully switched on. But I've heard the boss talking about who does it. One of your kind, a female elf or something, I think. A prisoner." The man paused, and I thought he might be done.

I tried to think of more questions, but he eventually opened his mouth again.

"But you'll never get into the place, even if you could find where they're being held. There's more guards than you've ever seen, and Jacobs himself designed the layout and security system."

His last sentence gave one thing away very clearly. He did know where the building was because he had seen how many guards there were himself.

His friends shouted so loudly after this that he shut his mouth and lifted his head imperiously, however.

I glanced at Ronan to see him still standing in the doorway. His face was expressionless. Now I was in a difficult spot. Could I get the other three to believe they would get better treatment if they told me more without removing Merl from his cage?

"Where's the building?" I asked as I tried to think.

"I told you, I don't know," Merl replied, and his friends relaxed a little.

"I don't believe you."

"Then go to hell, because I'm not telling you anything else," the man hissed through gritted teeth.

I frowned, banging up against the unexpected stopper in the flow of information. What was so bad about the location or his fear of a superior that he couldn't confirm where it was?

We can just follow a group back, Zephyr said in my head. *They've confirmed everything else they needed to.*

I sighed. Zephyr was right. It wasn't going to be as easy, but we could find Crawley's daughter another way.

CHAPTER SIXTEEN

I sat on a rooftop with Zephyr, eating as the sun sank. I marveled at how the elves had managed to sculpt something both living and made of the elements around them.

We were sitting on what looked like a large lily pad, the building underneath a mix of reddish sandstone and vines. Beyond us stretched the tops of many more buildings, each of them an individual work of art that complemented the whole.

Ronan was liaising with Lorcan while Zephyr and I caught up on a missed meal and made plans.

The prisoners had given us what little information they had, and it was clear we needed to follow the agents back to their base and hope it was obvious that was where Crawley's daughter was being held.

It also meant we could aid the Sanctuary that night as well. But I was worried. There were still a few unknowns.

Could Crawley fill in the gaps? Zephyr asked. *Especially if we told her Jacobs probably has her daughter and is using her to track down the Sanctuary?*

Maybe. If not, Erlan might be able to hack something. That kid has a way with computers I've never seen before.

We'll need to go back to LA, then.

I sighed. That was a lot of flying after a night on watch and tracking down agents as they went back to their bases.

We don't have a better plan.

No. And if we're going to infiltrate a base and try to rescue someone, I want our folks with us.

Then back to LA it is.

I frowned. It was sort of a plan. I was still shooting into the dark, but we knew more than we used to. Jacobs was definitely behind this, and it was highly likely he had Crawley's daughter.

Although I'd expected to paint a target on my back when I'd taken down the agency in LA and possibly have a few rogue agents band up and try to take us out at some point, I hadn't expected anyone to go after the Sanctuary. I'd not even expected most people to know about it.

It was clear more mythicals were feeling unsafe out in the world now, though, and many of them were finally talking about their heritage and reaching out to each other. In a lot of ways, it was a good thing that people were more aware of the Sanctuary and my dojo, but it brought dangers with it.

I also knew it wasn't a good idea to underestimate Jacobs. He clearly had a grudge and wasn't going to give up.

Right. Up, I thought as we finished the last of our food and drink. I gathered the large platters and my plate, cup, and Zephyr's bowls. It was time to get back to work.

Now standing up, I watched the last sliver of sun disappear and the colored clouds scud across the sky toward it as if they were trying to catch up.

Zephyr got up a moment later and shook and stretched. I felt a little tired, my body clock trying to tell me it was the end of a day, but we'd offered to help protect the Sanctuary, and from our perch, I could see the hundreds of lives that included, many others having been dining in the sun as it set as well.

I rushed down another spiral staircase made of vines near the base of the lily, and an elf I didn't recognize hurried over and took the dirty dishes from me.

I thanked her and smiled as she scurried away, putting them in a small cart before heading to the next house to collect more. I spotted the water master, Ruehnar, as Zephyr landed beside me, having jumped down from the roof.

"Aella!" he said. "I heard you were with us again for a short while. You look well, and I swear those ears of yours are a little more pointed than the last time we met. You must be making good use of your abilities."

I smiled and nodded. I'd thought the same, and Zephyr had confirmed on many occasions that embracing the elven nature within me was literally making me more elven. Something about the way elves used magic being the reason they lived longer and had different bodies.

It heavily implied that elves had once been human and the two races had digressed because of the use of magic, but it was a scientific theory Chris had suggested and I'd not entirely understood. It made no sense that my ears grew more pointed because of it if nothing else.

"How is your learning coming along? Any progress I should know about?" he asked.

I paused for a moment, thinking about how best to phrase my response.

"None in the magical sense, but I'm not great at growing things and..." I trailed off as I reached into the bag and pulled out the potted plant, complete with its safety covering. "This is doing pretty well, all things considered."

"Oh, that is sprouting well. You should take that to Orthelo, the earth master. He knows how difficult that plant is to grow. I believe it's not easy, and that's the point of it being one the students use. It'll only grow if you have some ability."

"With earth?" I asked.

He nodded, beaming. I was surprised by his reaction, thinking that he would have been disappointed that I hadn't managed to handle the water aspect.

I stared at the plant and then at him, and he chuckled.

"It's quite common for younger elves and students to use their abilities in an accidental way, and it can take years for it to become anything more than that, unless you get a high-pressure situation as you were subjected to with your wind abilities."

"Then I hope this means progress," I replied, suddenly a little more excited. Could this truly mean he was right and my lineage had given me the ability to control more than one element?

"As I said, go find the earth master. I'm sure he'll want to hear of this and have the chance to talk to you."

I nodded, listening as I was given directions and then hurrying that way. We had time for a five-minute chat, but little more. This didn't seem to be the kind of thing that could wait, however.

The earth master was exactly where we'd been told he would be, sitting in a large building surrounded by both plants and animals. I found him up a ladder, poring over a nest in a strange-looking tree. Near the base was a large furry dog of some kind, its ear torn and its stump of a tail thumping.

As I came closer, I could feel heat radiating off the tree and saw the sweat on the elf's face. I had to duck as a bird flew overhead and settled on the branch of another plant in the far corner. It landed beside another small fox-like creature with a bandage on its leg and attempted to comfort it.

"Ah, Aella, I believe?" the earth master asked before I could say anything.

I nodded as he came down the ladder and stared at the pot I carried.

"This is a lerianna plant, isn't it?" he asked, coming closer and examining it.

"I don't know. Ruehnar gave it to me in a pot as a seed about two months ago. Told me to come show you that it had grown."

The earth master had a grin on his face. He was no longer looking at the plant but me and Zephyr.

"Well, I must say, I don't usually like losing a bet, but Ruehnar was right. Two elements in one elf. My, my, I never thought I'd live to see it."

I frowned, not sure if I was pleased with the strange assessment. I'd not confirmed a single thing yet.

"Let me guess. You didn't do it deliberately, and you

don't know if you truly can control the earth and plants around you?" he asked.

"Something like that."

"Well, the lerianna plant is one of the hardest to grow. There's never been any point in giving a student something easy to do. We don't want someone thinking they're an earth elemental when they're not."

I blinked. Did this mean I *could* control another element?

"It will take time to learn to control it, and I would love to begin helping you right now, but I've only recently received the phoenix egg in this nest here, and unless I can get it warm enough while still in its nest, it will never hatch."

I raised my eyebrows, but the earth master turned away and scurried back up his ladder. Although I'd expected more of a fanfare at the news that I could control two elements, it was clear the elf cared deeply for a great number of animals. I had been dismissed.

After giving one of the fluffy creatures near the door a head rub, I made my way back out of the makeshift animal hospital with Zephyr in tow.

Still possessing more than one question but with my mood boosted, we went to join Ronan at the log cabin on the border of the Sanctuary. When we arrived, Lorcan was with him, and it made me wonder if I'd interrupted something. Both smiled as Zephyr and I approached, however.

"We've identified the key locations the agents target," Ronan said as we stopped in front of them. "Lorcan is going to take an extra team to one of them and has asked me to take one to the second. Would you be willing to periodically fly between them and act as backup and extra eyes around the edge in case more show up?"

"Sounds like a plan," I replied, having expected something similar. I didn't want to be part of the normal guard contingent because I wanted to be able to follow one of the groups back to their base, but equally, I wanted to be able to defend where needed. This allowed them to use me most effectively while I still kept my long-term agenda.

"We'll head out in about an hour, when it really gets dark. Feel free to prepare whatever food and drink you want for quick pit stops, and drop off anything you want to keep safe at the cabin," Lorcan added, eyeing my bag. It was a good idea, so I made my way inside and prepared a large slow-cooker of casserole that could sit and keep itself going for whoever wanted to drop in and grab some.

With that done, I unpacked some of the unnecessary stuff from my bag and put my plant in a safe corner, then added back the snacks, some bottles of water, and a few other useful nighttime tools like rope and flashlights. I wasn't sure what I'd need but knew I'd be out a long time and would probably meet some agents along the way, so I packed tranq darts and one of the guns we'd liberated from the agents in the past.

I didn't use them as much now that I could control Zephyr's breath and move it, since it was more potent than the tranqs. Having a dragon with me was a serious advantage in any fight these days.

Ready? I asked Zephyr as I did up the bag.

Sure. Not like I bring anything with me but you.

We should get you some saddlebags, I replied. I grinned as I imagined him wearing a leather bag on each side of his large body. He brought his eyebrows lower and nearer the middle, the closest thing he could do to a frown.

You could put snacks in them. Maybe even pizza.

Tilting his head to the side, he considered the suggestion seriously, and I laughed. Food could get him to do almost anything.

Without another word about the silly idea, we rejoined Ronan and made our way out of the hut toward the point his group had decided to defend. They stopped about five hundred meters out, still able to see the edge of the Sanctuary, although any agents who got that far wouldn't be able to. It looked like the desert continued for miles behind us.

With Ronan was an elf I recognized from previous guard duties, the dwarf who'd greeted us the first time we'd arrived at this Sanctuary location, another centaur, and to my surprise, the water elf who tended the farms and had helped us put out the forest fire the first time we'd been at the Sanctuary.

"Good evening, Aella," Gwaelon said immediately. "You look well, all events considered."

"As do you," I replied, hoping it didn't sound trite. "I hope you have not had too much work to do, bringing water to this barren region."

"It's not without its challenges, but it gives the brain a reason to stay young and active."

"It is likely to be tested tonight," Ronan replied. "We should spread out and find cover. It would not benefit the Sanctuary to be seen by the agents before we see them and have a chance to deter them from their path."

"Noted," Gwaelon replied, heading to the right toward a bush that would provide adequate cover.

"We'll hang back," I added since I was not part of their defense crew and was aware I'd need to get in the air in less than half an hour. We'd worked out earlier that it took about fifteen minutes to fly between the two encampments of guards. With half an hour at the camps, we'd only be gone from each one for an hour.

Anything could happen in that time, but it would keep us on our toes. It made me feel like we were helping, even if we were only acting as messengers with tidings of quiet and calm to begin with.

Half an hour later we were in the air, having left Ronan's group to wait in the dark. It was now pitch-black and cloudy. Few stars were out, and the moon was currently obscured.

Zephyr could still see well enough to travel around the perimeter, the occasional hut or lookout post going by beneath us. It was peaceful, but I ached a little after the long flight the previous night.

We need to practice flying longer distances, I said as I spotted Lorcan and we prepared to land and report.

I think we already are, Zephyr replied.

I stifled a chuckle as we came down between Lorcan and the Sanctuary dome and hunkered down for a moment to check that the coast was clear so we could approach.

After erecting a sound barrier in front of Lorcan to hide the obvious signs of our movement, I crept toward him and gave my report. He nodded while I talked.

"Same here," he replied. "Hang back and move on when

you need to. I don't expect any different for another hour or two yet."

"Noted." It was clear Lorcan was a centaur of few words, so I kept mine brief. As I slipped back toward Zephyr, I spotted Seth hiding behind another bush. He wasn't looking my way, but his fists were clenched, and I could have sworn I could feel air moving toward him. Had he been listening in on our conversation somehow?

I wasn't sure what element he controlled. He'd assumed he would be able to bond with Zephyr but had reported to the fire element master at the training sessions I'd seen him at.

I could only wonder at the answers. I didn't plan to strike up a conversation with the grumpy elf.

I mostly stood near the border with Zephyr, getting progressively more bored before we flew on again. And then again half an hour later.

At this rate, it was going to be a long night, but as I joined Ronan for the third time, there was activity in the distance. Two agents were approaching, clearly trying to sneak through the grasses.

Head behind them, and we'll try yesterday's tactics again, I suggested to Zephyr.

We swooped in from behind, and I prepared to control Zephyr's gas weapon. Although we wanted them to retreat so we could follow, this early in the night, knocking them out was a better idea. We needed to defend the Sanctuary from other attackers, and we could still follow them when they woke up.

Zephyr inhaled and readied to breathe his gas in their direction as we came closer and dropped in much the same way as the night before. Just before Zephyr could exhale, one of the agents either heard something or acted on his sixth sense because he looked behind him.

"Dragon," he called before grabbing his partner and trying to pull him to one side. Zephyr exhaled anyway, too late to stop himself, and I leaned to one side so I could see both the cloud of gas and the agents as we flew overhead.

I locked my mind onto the vapor, moving it closer and catching one of them in the face. Not sure of the other, I could only look behind and hope. Ronan came forward from his hiding place, a tranquilizer gun in his hands after the training Daisy had given him.

He didn't fire it, however, and we swung back around to find I had managed to take out both targets with Zephyr's breath weapon after all. When Ronan reached them, we landed as well. Gwaelon came up a moment later.

"Going to be an easy night if you swoop in like that and knock these humans out before they can get close enough for some action," Gwaelon said. His words sounded like an admonishment, but the smile on his face suggested otherwise.

"I'll move them farther away," I replied. "But keep an eye on them. At some point, they'll wake up again. Should be more than three hours, but we don't know how much longer than that."

"I'll call if they awaken," Ronan replied. "Or keep them busy until you can return and follow them back to their offices."

I nodded and thanked them before we all went back to our usual positions. I'd only been there for a few seconds before Ronan looked straight at me and motioned for me to head to the right.

For a moment, I didn't know what he was trying to say, but Zephyr leaped into the air, and Ronan's eyes flickered as he slipped into a trance. A minute later, he repeated the action.

Lorcan needed us, but we were fifteen minutes away.

CHAPTER SEVENTEEN

We flew as quickly as we could to Lorcan's team, considering going through the Sanctuary rather than around, but Ronan had asked us to go around, and we were keeping an eye on the perimeter in other places too. It was possible someone in another position needed us more than Lorcan.

Onward we flew until the reason for our early flight came into view. There were agents everywhere, and they had clearly tried to overrun the guards. Lorcan and his team had come around to the left of their original position and joined two guards from other stations, but there were still more agents than mythicals.

They're acting strangely, Zephyr said in my head as we flew closer, still too far away to do much.

It was soon obvious that the soldiers were pulling back if engaged and then walking farther out before rushing in again from a another position.

They're just trying to get past and into the Sanctuary, I replied. *We have to keep them out.*

Zephyr dived at the nearest moving figure, an agent who had snuck around even farther. I knocked him off his feet with a blast of air as Zephyr prepared to exhale.

The air hit the agent instantly, but no sooner was that one down and unconscious than another appeared, this one clutching an orb. I blasted the precious stone out of his hand as we flew overhead, unable to do more for a moment.

"What took you so long?" Seth called. He appeared from nowhere and punched the agent to keep him down before pocketing the orb. Another agent came out from behind a bush, pulling out a weapon of some kind.

"The information I had wasn't clear about the location. I had to fly around the edge and make sure the perimeter was safe," I said as I slid off Zephyr's back and landed in front of Seth, deflecting a bullet meant for him. "And you might want to stop yelling."

Seth shut his mouth with a snap, the shock of me having just saved his life and the danger his taunt had put him in making him listen for once. Not saying another word, I blasted the agent off his feet and slammed him into the base of a nearby cactus without realizing what it was until the agent screamed in pain.

I winced and pulled him back off, but he no doubt had more than a few thorns sticking out of his flesh. While it served him right, I felt guilty. I avoided killing people or causing them unnecessary pain if I could, especially those who were just following orders. Even if I didn't agree with them.

Moving on, I reached for Zephyr with my mind for an

update on potential positions. I saw Zephyr swoop over-head again and heard him exhale not too far away.

There's about nine more active agents I can spot, but just when I think I can see them all, another appears out from behind a bush or cactus and I lose track of the others again.

It wasn't useful information, but we had to do the best we could. I took to the air again and Zephyr directed me to the nearest agent he could see and went after another. Chaos ensued while I tried to spar in the dark with an agent who just wanted to get past me. Eventually I pulled my tranq gun and shot him.

The second I was sure I'd hit my target, I blasted into the air and to one side, expecting return fire. I dodged it just in time, a bullet hitting the ground not far from my previous position and sending the sandy red dirt into the sky.

I was about to head for my attacker when Seth hit the female agent with a fireball from behind. She panicked, dropped her gun, and started rolling in the dirt. The fire spread to a small plant nearby as Seth tried to slink away from the bright patch and leave the agent to me.

Zephyr flew in, gassing her as she tried to stand again, but the edge of the vapor hit the burning greenery and caused a reaction I hadn't expected. Fire rolled through the vapor, engulfing the woman. She let out a pained squeal but collapsed anyway.

As the fire died, I dared to get closer.

I assume you didn't know your breath could do that, I said to Zephyr.

A water elf appeared after a moment, dousing the flames and disappearing into the darkness again. A few seconds later, Zephyr flew overhead and behind me before pouncing on another agent.

The agent let out a surprised yell as Zephyr carried him back the way he'd come.

No, I didn't, Zephyr said as he dropped the agent. There was a crunch when he landed in a bush, followed by a groan.

I finally reached the agent we'd singed and tried to examine her in the dark. She had a pulse, but her breathing was a little wheezy.

The idea that we might have collectively burned her lungs came to mind, but it had been an accident. From the shocked look on Seth's face as he retreated, it was clear he hadn't been expecting it either.

Listening to everything around me and feeling for movement in the air, I detected something slow-moving even farther to my left and took off toward it. I was rewarded by crashing headlong into another agent far sooner than I'd expected and taking us both down in a tangle of limbs.

The man tried to pull a knife, but my body reacted instinctively. My karate training took over as I disarmed him and knocked him out with a hard punch. Reaching for the air again, I tried to find the sneak nearby.

At first I couldn't detect anything, and I imagined the agent keeping still and listening as well, spooked by the sounds of fighting nearby. Closing my eyes, I tried to feel even more clearly and farther out. I became aware of Lorcan or another centaur somewhere behind and to my right.

To the left and closer to the Sanctuary, I finally felt the

agent move again. Once more, I ran for my quarry, doing what I could to block my sound so they wouldn't know I was coming.

As I got closer, however, they sped up and sprinted toward the perimeter, clutching a glowing orb. I aimed to head them off, but they were running fast, the dull light of the orb they held low revealing that they had night vision goggles on their head, pushed up now that they knew where they were going. They must have seen me coming.

Pushing myself even faster with my air powers, I began to gain on them, but even at the top speed I could run while boosted, I didn't catch them before they made it over the boundary. Their eyes went wide and they slowed as the view changed.

I remembered how awed I had been when I'd first seen the Sanctuary, and it was particularly beautiful at night, with all the lights and fires that danced and lit up the plant life and natural stone houses.

The agent tried to get away from me by heading back out of the city. Knowing I couldn't let them report back with the whereabouts of the Sanctuary, I pushed myself and hit them at full speed.

The contact stung me, my forehead hitting their chin and one of my knees connecting with a softer, more fleshy part. I was grateful I'd had a slight barrier to keep me from some of the harm, but he (the fleshy part told me that) was flung off his feet, his arm at a strange angle.

I noticed his pocket bulging with a spherical light, no doubt another orb. The agent groaned where he landed, one hand going up to his chin while the other hung limp beside him.

After snatching the orb out of his pocket, I stepped back and frowned again. I kept hurting people far worse than I intended.

These agents are helping a maniac wipe out this entire city. They don't deserve your pity, Zephyr said into my head as he pinned down another and exhaled gas into the man's face.

Maybe, but I want to take the high road when I can. I don't want to hurt anyone who doesn't have to be hurt.

You're not.

It was reassuring, but I still felt guilty as I blasted another agent off his feet with air and an elf knocked him out. Lorcan appeared at my side a moment later, panting. He had a cut on his flank, although it wasn't deep.

"I think that's the last of them," he said as the night went quiet, the only sound the moaning of the agent I'd hurt.

Zephyr knocked him out a moment later—a mercy, really. Holding out the orb to Lorcan, I tried to calm my racing heart and rapid breathing.

I helped pull the agents away from the Sanctuary border, with the exception of the two who had crossed in. Seth and Lorcan cuffed them and instructed a dwarf to fetch medics and a guard unit to take them, tend to them, and then lock them up along with the others.

"You should continue with your patrol," Lorcan said to me as soon as the agents were far enough away.

I was only too grateful to pull back from the tiring fighting. While it hadn't felt as dangerous as some of the other battles I'd been in—after all, I'd only been shot at a couple of times—it was stressful, and I'd relied on my powers heavily.

As I walked beside Zephyr, I ate a granola bar.

I have a feeling this is going to be a long night, I said so only he'd hear me.

So far, so good.

These agents won't give up, and only one needs to sneak through our net and get back home for Jacobs to have the exact location of the Sanctuary.

True, but we made a difference tonight, and that's all we can do.

I sighed, grateful for how calm Zephyr always was, even in difficult situations and facing unknown amounts of danger. With all his ancestral memories, it was probably just another day of being a dragon, but I still appreciated his presence like no other.

We were soon in the air again, the night once more calm as we flew in circles and paused to watch our friends' backs now and then.

Several more hours passed, and we stopped for food at the midway point, grateful for the short break even though we ate it where we could see those on watch with Ronan.

Not much later, we were in the air again and flying around. We found Lorcan and his group eating as well, and I dropped down for another brief on the situation while Zephyr watched the horizon far better than the rest of us could.

"Some of the agents from earlier came around for another try a few hundred meters to our right, but we got their orb off them and sent them packing," Lorcan said. "I don't expect to be bothered again tonight."

"That's a relief," I replied, stifling another yawn. There had not been enough sleep in the last forty-eight hours of my life.

I was pretty sure Lorcan smiled and gave a slight incline of his head the same way Ronan did when he was showing his respect for something I'd said. The help we'd given him must have begun warming the older centaur to me finally.

Before Seth could make a remark, I moved back and found a perch in a sturdy bush to take the weight off my legs and keep watch for a bit.

If Lorcan was confident he would be safe and we'd seen little in the way of other attempts on the Sanctuary, I was pretty sure we could move on to the second part of our plan—following agents back to their base, where we'd hopefully find Crawley's daughter.

I informed Lorcan I might not be back as we flew off but didn't commit either way. The safety of the Sanctuary had to come first.

"Don't worry about us. You've already given us a considerable advantage against the agents compared to previous nights. It would also benefit us to know where their base is. The council is considering launching an attack of our own, but to do that, we'd need to know what we were targeting."

"There will be no need," I replied without hesitation. "If I'm right about how they're getting this far, I'll be able to solve the problem for you."

Lorcan hesitated before bowing.

"I hope you're right. I do not relish the idea of taking my unit into a battle with an enemy that is this violent and disrespectful of the value of life."

I bowed back, sharing the sentiment. It felt like it had been a long time since I could be safe in the knowledge that they were only trying to knock me out and transport me somewhere else or incarcerate me. For months now, Jacobs had authorized the use of lethal force.

Feeling like we'd been relieved of our earlier duty, Zephyr and I agreed to fly the shorter route back to Ronan, despite it being the wrong way around the border. We were running a small risk, but given the time and Lorcan's expectations, I didn't feel guilty.

As Ronan came into sight, battling with an agent in hand-to-hand combat, I felt like we'd made the right decision. His unit was in shambles, the water elf, Gwaelon, holding back two agents alone while the dwarf tended to someone else.

Hurry, I told Zephyr needlessly.

I tensed as I reached for the air to try to help. I smacked any agents I could see with the forces I could muster quickly. It gave Ronan the advantage he needed to best the agent he fought and stopped two more from sneaking past the boundaries, but the latter relief was only temporary.

As Zephyr made his way toward one of the agents, I blasted off his back and into the other.

We both went down in a tangle of limbs, then I used my enhanced fighting skills to overpower them. Ronan appeared at my side a moment later, distracting me.

I took a punch to the jaw that knocked me back and made me see stars. A powerful hoof slammed into the agent's arm before he could hit me again. I heard a sickening crunch, but the agent only grunted.

I scurried to my feet, ready to defend and attack once more. Instead of engaging us further, the agent looked at us and then over my shoulder before he stepped back.

"Retreat back to base," he yelled. "Head back to base."

I stayed where I was, rubbing my jaw, but we needed to follow if we could. Everyone else was done now the Sanctuary had been defended.

"One got into the Sanctuary and then got away," Gwaelon said as he came running up, a bandage around his middle. "It was one of the agents from earlier. He woke up while we were fighting and snuck right past me."

"He needs to be stopped," Ronan replied. "If he gets back to their base, he could lead a whole army here."

"On it," I replied, pushing up into the air again. Zephyr followed, catching me before propelling us both after the agents.

Several shots rang out from somewhere, and Zephyr swerved. A bullet hit him hard enough that he grunted.

You okay? I asked, knowing he had softer underscales that were not bulletproof.

Just about. But we're going to need to figure out where those bullets are coming from.

I sighed. Zephyr was right, but it was a distraction we didn't need. I concentrated on the flow of the air out from us, pinpointing the source of the movement as the bullets whistled toward us. Satisfied I knew where the snipers were, I directed Zephyr toward the first of the pair with my thoughts.

We moved as one, dropping down on the first shooter as he tried to run. Zephyr exhaled, and I pushed the cloud around the short but sturdy woman's head. She held her breath, but I kept the gas moving with her until she went down.

I quickly felt for the air movement of the second, the

other agent now running as well. Repeating the flight and descent onto the target, we landed again and gassed that one too.

By the time we'd dealt with these agents, the rest were out of range of both sight and my abilities. We'd lost them thanks to a couple of snipers who appeared to have been placed for exactly this eventuality.

What do you want to do? Zephyr asked. I imagined what fate might befall the Sanctuary if the agents came back with an army.

I don't know.

CHAPTER EIGHTEEN

Flying around, Zephyr and I tried to find the agents again, but we'd lost them. Fear for the Sanctuary gripped my chest and made it hard to breathe. How could we have lost them?

Stopping them was part of our job.

What about that base we flew over on the way here? Zephyr asked a moment later. *We're not far from it.*

I paused, my heart stopping with realization. Of course. We knew about a likely base already.

Head straight there, I replied, funneling my abilities into making us as fast as possible despite how tired I was. At the same time, I reached into my bag's side pocket and pulled out another granola bar.

It wasn't easy to eat it while flying so fast, but I only lost a few small pieces while I munched it down, taking big bites.

When the lights appeared ahead of us, it didn't take long to make out the moving cars and people coming and going. It looked like Zephyr had guessed correctly, and this was where the agents had come from.

He lifted higher and we slowed as we drew closer, but we still needed to see well enough to confirm the presence of agents we recognized from the night's encounters. I created a sound barrier and hoped no one looked up as we swept over the top.

It's the same agents, Zephyr said as he banked to come around the other way.

Land. We can sneak closer more easily on foot.

Zephyr didn't head down right away but flew to one edge of the base, where there were fewer lights and cameras and a tall metal fence. It was where we'd be least expected, but it puzzled me. Most of the agents were on the opposite side of the grounds.

Best place to get inside the perimeter, Zephyr explained as we dropped down beyond the fence and just outside camera range.

I nodded, but it didn't stop me from worrying that we might miss something important. I kept us wrapped in a sound bubble, however, and hurried with Zephyr toward the darkest section of fence. While there, I moved the cameras with my abilities, using air to push each one up. It took a while, but we were finally clear to move.

Looking both ways to check that we were alone, I tried to figure out how we'd get inside. A moment later, Zephyr flew over the fence, narrowly missing the rolled barbed wire on the top that was installed to lean outward and deter people from climbing in.

I rolled my eyes at the simplicity of it and how I'd forgotten we could both fly.

Still keeping any sounds from traveling out from us, I lifted myself up and followed, taking care not to get as near the hazardous fence. Before long, I was standing beside him, and we were looking for either Crawley's daughter or the agent who had passed the Sanctuary barrier.

Several sentries were patrolling the yard in seemingly random patterns, which meant we needed to consider how we would get farther than the end of the building we were standing beside.

Use my paralysis gas, Zephyr suggested. *Sneak it up to them, and they'll just go to sleep for a bit.*

Perfect, I replied, grinning.

Sneaking around wasn't something I'd have thought we'd be good at, but it was surprisingly easy now I could control his breath weapon and stop the sound we made from traveling too far. It still wouldn't be easy for us to get where we wanted to go, though. There were tens of agents on the base, if not hundreds.

When I took out a pair of patrolling guards and they slumped to the ground, it drew the attention of a nearby sentry in a tower. He reached for what looked like a radio.

Shitsticks.

I'd not planned to take them all out at once.

As I moved the gas cloud closer, I jetted a small gust of wind at the hand holding the radio. He fumbled and dropped it, buying me time to move the gas up and envelope the distracted sentry's head.

Within seconds he was no longer a threat.

That was close, Zephyr said, his voice as full of relief as I felt.

Tell me about it. I need to make a mental note to do a whole set at the same time and make sure no one can see it.

We should hide the agents we've dealt with, too. Don't want another patrol finding bodies.

Good point.

Using up even more energy, I lifted all three fallen agents and floated them up and over the fence before depositing them behind a bush. Zephyr chuckled.

What? I asked.

They're going to be confused when they can move again.

It'll be morning by then, and we'll be long gone. For the next few minutes, we were unchallenged by any obstacles, but we still stopped to listen by doorways and try to work out what was inside each building.

We passed a couple of what looked like labs, but I couldn't be sure. I didn't think we would be interested in anything inside the buildings either way.

The next corner we came to revealed a building with a lot more activity and interest. We could now see the edge of the parking lot and the entrance to one of the larger buildings. This one had two sets of guards outside it, a thumb pad to scan in authorized personnel, and several sentries in towers who could see the entrance and the parking lot well.

There were also a lot more lights in this area, and there was no way we were going to be able to move through it without taking out every agent we could see at once.

I was just trying to work out how many agents that might be when more appeared and hurried up to the doors to the main building.

"Is the boss still inside?" one asked, his face familiar. It was one of the pair of agents who had been knocked out and then snuck away. One or both of them would now be able to see the Sanctuary wherever it was.

I reached for some more air to blast them all off their feet, but my head started to pound. I couldn't stop them all at once that way, and I couldn't gas this many agents at once either, not even if Zephyr exhaled several times so I could create plenty of little bubbles of paralyzing gas.

There are just too many of them, Zephyr said. *We should retreat and warn the Sanctuary. They'll need as much time as possible to move somewhere else.*

But we can't just leave. We told the Sanctuary we'd protect them.

And we have to the best of our current ability. While the Sanctuary is moving, we can head to LA and get Minsheng and the others. With some help, we may be able to take on the agents here, but not alone.

I clenched my jaw and fists, wanting to fight, but my body was so exhausted I couldn't even do that for long. We were going to have to do as Zephyr suggested.

The council wasn't going to like it, however.

They'll get over it. Might even encourage more of them to take a stand rather than hide, Zephyr replied, sounding grumpy. It made me feel a little better that he was as annoyed at the situation as I was.

Within minutes we were back where we'd started, on the other side of the fence and in the dark.

I used the last of my energy to move the three agents we'd placed outside back into the positions we'd knocked them out in and then started walking back to the Sanctuary.

Although it would have been quicker to fly, I didn't have the energy to get into the air, and I strongly suspected Zephyr was almost as tired. I ripped open some more granola bars, giving Zephyr a couple even though they were a mouthful to him, and chowed down on two myself.

I hope there's some more of that casserole, Zephyr said a moment later.

It made me chuckle, and soon the pair of us were laughing at the absurdity of our lives. By the time we'd calmed, we had a little more energy and got ourselves in the air.

Zephyr flew us back to the log cabin, and we made our report to Ronan.

"I'm sorry. I didn't get there in time. I—"

"You did all you could, Aella," Ronan cut me off and echoed what Zephyr had said. "No one has lost their life this night, due in part to your efforts. That is a success of its own, and we now have warning of what will follow. I'm sure the council will agree that moving once more is best, as you've already suggested."

"I will suggest it, as well," Lorcan said, walking out of the darkness.

I opened my mouth to apologize once more, but Lorcan put a hand on my shoulder and nodded at me.

"Your aid was greatly appreciated this night. Zephyr and you helped the Sanctuary survive yet again. I think we should inform the council as quickly as possible and begin moving."

"We flew over many good locations on the way here," I replied. "We'll stick around until you're out of the area and then head back to LA and put together a team. We're going to infiltrate the base anyway. Hopefully they'll be too busy dealing with us to even attempt to look for the Sanctuary again."

"Once again, you offer us more help than we would dare ask for. I was skeptical that an heir of one of the great elves had come to us when you first appeared, but it's clear that my doubts were unfounded. Rest until we have need of you. Ronan and I will convince the council that what you suggest is best."

I nodded, too shocked by his declaration of faith to know how to reply.

Rest sounded like a great idea, however, even if I felt guilty that I wasn't going to go before the council. Seth appeared before I could head into the cabin and back up to the room made especially for us, however.

Ronan and Lorcan excused themselves, almost as if they had expected the elf to appear and have something to say. Too tired for a fight or the usual antagonism, I considered asking him to wait to say whatever he wanted to say later, but I held my tongue. He'd sought me out. He must have had a good reason.

He watched the centaurs leave and then looked down. There was none of his usual bravado in his pose. His shoulders were slumped, and his eyes looked as tired as my own probably did.

"Thank you," he said. "You saved our lives earlier. You saved mine. I let my grudge make me stupid, and rather than leave me to suffer the consequences, you put yourself in harm's way to make sure I lived."

"I did. Because no matter whether we like each other or agree with each other, we're on the same team. All those agents care about is destroying or capturing mythicals so we can't make them feel scared of our potential. That makes you my ally."

He let his head drop again and gulped. I wasn't sure if he had more to say, so I waited.

"I'm starting to see why you're the one with the only dragon on the planet," he said. "I can't say I'll agree with you in future, and I still think we should be hiding because we aren't ready for the whole world to know about us, but it's clear you're formidable and here to help."

"I might have made the wrong decision, outing us like I did, but we can't undo it now. And I did what I thought was right at the time. It's all any of us can do. But I need to rest now. The Sanctuary is going to be moving soon, and then I need to put together a team and rescue a mythical from the agents."

"They've got someone?"

"A half-elf, I think."

"I'd like to help."

I blinked, then nodded.

"Get some sleep then, and stick close to Ronan. When we're ready to mount a rescue, I'll let him know, and you can meet us. But if you come to help, you'll be following my orders or his, understand? Even if you disagree, we'll be trying not to attract attention and will need to act quickly. Hesitation and disobedience could get us and her killed."

"I can handle that for a mission, especially to help a fellow elf." With that, Seth left.

Watching him go, I felt strangely mixed. Part of me wanted to keep disliking him, but he'd done a brave thing by coming to me, and I couldn't fault his desire to help others.

And so our team grows, Zephyr said as we made our way up to our room.

At this point, given what we're up against, the more, the merrier.

Plus, it means we can set fire to some more stuff. Payback for the warehouse burning up.

I grinned as we settled down beside each other. Although we'd already demolished one agency building as payback, I liked the sound of dealing with a second.

Seth and you could work together, I added a moment later as I had an idea. *And Erlan and I could make fiery tornadoes.*

I think those are called firenadoes.

Whatever they're called, it's going to burn that place to the ground.

After we've rescued the mythical.

Of course. We don't want crispy elf, just wrecked buildings.

Mmmm, crispy duck...

My mouth watered, and Zephyr's stomach rumbled.

As soon as everyone is rescued and safe, we'll eat an entire Chinese banquet. Deal?

Deal.

CHAPTER NINETEEN

In the air once more, I watched the nomadic line of mythicals head toward their new destination. At first I'd worried that they would struggle to pack and move everything in even a couple of days, but the elves had worked as efficient teams, and now I was flying above them all on Zephyr's back.

The mythicals' line consisted of far more cars than I'd expected and even a few army vehicles like the one Ronan had acquired for us. Everyone else rode animals or brought heavily laden carriages and carts pulled by horses and beasts I'd never encountered. Two larger beasts carried a tank of water with the aquatic mythicals safely stowed inside.

There were two divisions to the caravan. Those who could travel fastest in the vehicles were going ahead to set up the new Sanctuary, and those who needed to move at a pace all the animals could match made their way as best they could. For the moment, we were flying above the second, helping them get farther away from the agent base in safety.

The sun had only been in the sky for a few hours, and we'd had at best about four hours' sleep, but a hearty breakfast and the information Ronan had given us while we ate had seen us on the road along with the entire Sanctuary.

Now I could see them all, I was in awe of how many there were. While I'd known the Sanctuary held at least a hundred elves of various degrees of lineage and ability, I hadn't realized there were a similar number of dwarves and even more gnomes.

I counted only about twenty centaurs, but they were all strong men and women who helped wherever they could. And then there were the mixed races and the ones I didn't have names for. In total, there must have been more than a thousand of them.

We'd also flown over the agent base from up high a couple of times and checked the activity levels. It was quieter this morning but not empty of agents going here and there. It was clearly mostly agents, their suits and cars easily distinguishable from the others.

Guards still stood outside the main building as well, and there appeared to be a few more patrols and sentries than there had been. No doubt because they'd realized that they'd not been alone during the night.

As the caravan got farther away from the agents, I grew bored. We were traveling a strange route, and the group of people had a small protective barrier around them that kept others from them, so the danger was minimal anyway.

Eventually, we swooped down to land beside Ronan.

"If we don't leave soon, we won't have time to get to LA and then back to the agency base before nightfall," I said.

"You've already done plenty to aid us," Ronan replied. "Go, and I'll join you on the way back."

"Seth wishes to come too," I reminded him before we got into the sky again.

Ronan bowed, and I turned to wave at him before Zephyr spread his wings and sped away.

The journey back during the day made me think we were flying over a whole new part of the world. Everything looked different in the daytime, and we hit rain a few times and had to fly through it.

Thankfully the slipstream effect I created helped keep most of the water off too, but we were still drenched in no time. We were moving too fast to avoid all that water.

The caravan was traveling west, so there was less distance to cover, but we were significantly more tired to start with.

Within an hour, we'd had to land and take a break. I took the opportunity to find us some food, getting Zephyr to stop near a store so I could refill my bag with snacks and buy us something to eat.

I was low on cash so it was nothing fancy, but I didn't doubt that Minsheng or Daisy would feed us when we got back to the dojo.

Another two stops and we were finally coming up on LA, the city on the horizon and stretching out before us. Once again it felt like coming home, and I was reminded that I'd finally settled somewhere. I'd run so many times in the past. Now I could be safe in the knowledge I wasn't running anymore. Not even when I so easily could and had a big list of reasons to do so.

We landed on the roof, as always, and I called out to announce our arrival. Some of the fire salamanders came running up to us, and I made a fuss of them while I rested.

They soon scurried off and Erlan appeared, carrying a laptop.

"How's it going?" I asked, motioning to the device he was carrying.

"I've managed to find a few things. Some files on us, but nothing very interesting or that we don't already know. I've exchanged a couple of messages with the previous owner. She's very concerned, and I had to reassure her that you were looking for her daughter despite the lack of communication. You *are* looking for her daughter, right?"

I nodded.

"Not only that, I think I've found her daughter," I replied. "If you could tell her we plan to rescue her tonight if she's where I think she is, I'd appreciate it."

"Consider it done. And it sounds like you've got a story to tell."

I grinned and nodded as Zephyr and I hurried past. We hadn't got very far when Minsheng come our way. He sighed with relief when he saw us.

"You look like you got wet. I hope you didn't try to fly through a storm."

"Not exactly a storm," I said, coming down the stairs just ahead of Zephyr. "I tried to use my abilities to keep it off, but it wasn't the easiest."

"I hope you don't get sick."

"Me too." I stopped in front of Minsheng. "We need to gather everyone and talk."

"You've got information, then?" he asked as we made our way through the building.

"I've got a target, and we're going to hit it tonight."

Minsheng lifted his eyebrows but didn't ask any more questions. Instead, he rushed off to get everyone else in the building.

Within ten minutes, we were all sitting around the dining table or leaning against walls, doorways, and mythicals. There were more faces than I'd expected. All three gnomes we'd rescued before I left were still here, and Lyra had joined us. Holfin had brought a friend, someone he wanted Daisy to meet.

We filled them in on everything we'd been up to, although I left out the dangerous details like almost being shot. It wasn't easy to keep them quiet while I talked, but eventually the group was informed and ready to decide how to handle the next part of the plan.

"It sounds like Crawley's daughter is there," Minsheng said. "But I must admit, it's risky not to be sure."

"I can try to get it confirmed," Erlan offered. "And you can fill me in on the rest of the plan on the way there."

I nodded and let the eager young elf head off once more to hack the computers. Chris shook his head but smiled at the retreating mythical.

The offer broke the ice, and they were all offering support, equipment, and abilities until we had something resembling a plan.

"And I guess I'm getting left here again," Lyra said once the room had gone silent.

"Someone needs to keep an eye on this place while we're gone," I replied. "And you won't be alone."

"No, I've got the injured and the weak." She pouted, but the look soon disappeared. "Don't worry, I understand. In a lot of ways, I should be grateful I'm involved in this at all, but I won't deny that it's hard to be human and watch you go off and have all the fun."

Several of the others got up as Lyra spoke, leaving to fetch equipment and belongings for a night raid. Although Zephyr and I could fly over the fence, the others would need a way in, and we'd have to set up some diversions. We also had to get Crawley's daughter out, and we didn't know how injured she was.

I was trying to think of something suitable to say to Lyra that might make her feel better when there was a knock on the front door. Frowning, I went toward reception, motioning for the others to stay back. It was too early in the day for dojo students.

My mouth fell open when I spotted Crawley. At least, I was pretty sure it was her. She was dressed in a thick coat and wore a scarf, glasses, and a hat pulled down over her face. Her hands were shoved into her pockets, and it was clear she was trying to look like anyone but herself.

I hurried to let her in.

"You've found her?" Crawley asked as she stepped away from the entrance, her voice confirming it was her.

"I think so. It's the only thing that makes sense, given what the agents the Sanctuary captured told me and what Jacobs has been up to. We're about to go rescue her."

"I want to come," she said.

I opened my mouth to refuse, and began shaking my

head. I'd already had Seth invite himself along, and Lyra was upset about not joining us.

Only a couple of months earlier, Crawley had been the enemy—an agent herself. Government people had hunted me in the past on her orders. There was no part of me that wanted her to come.

She reached for my arm and our eyes met, and I knew I couldn't say no. This was her daughter, and it was clear she loved the half-elf.

"All right," I replied. "You can help us, but I expect you to follow orders. And you'll have to wait patiently for the rest of us to get ready to head out. We've got a lot of ground to cover, and we've already decided on our plan and schedule. It's not going to change now, for better or worse."

She nodded, and I directed her toward the kitchen to wait. Zephyr came close as she walked away.

That was mature of you, Zephyr said.

How so?

You could easily have been petty. But we know she's formidable. You've even fought her once already and struggled to prevent her from achieving her goal.

I knew Zephyr was referring to the clash we'd had over an orb. Having him praise my maturity meant even more to me, however, especially given that he now remembered so many of his ancestors' experiences.

We've got to win over the world somehow, right? I replied. *Got to start with each and every person when we get the opportunity.*

News of Crawley's presence spread through the inhabitants of the dojo. Not all of them understood the significance of her joining us, but Minsheng appeared and went to talk to her.

Although I wanted to listen to him warn her not to screw me over or hurt me ever again, I opted to get some quiet time with Zephyr instead.

We wouldn't be flying for long on the way back, just at the beginning to get to the Sanctuary first and pick up Ronan, Seth, and anyone else intending to help us ready, and then at the end to get into position before the attack.

The rest of the time, we were going to have to ride inside our armored vehicle. It wasn't likely to be as comfortable as before. Zephyr was larger than ever, and it didn't give him much wriggle room anymore. It was all we had, however, and we needed to be hidden to head out there.

Over the next half-hour, everyone returned, Daisy among the first.

As she often did when she felt at a loose end and didn't know how to help, she started cooking, and I left Zephyr to play with the fire salamanders while I joined her in the kitchen.

"I remember the first time you ate with us," Daisy said. "You were such a shy young woman, a small dragon practically sitting on your lap, and you wanted very little other than to be left alone. Now look at you, rescuing others, providing protection, and leading this little army."

"It seems surreal, doesn't it?" I replied, peeling another onion and trying not to get it too close to my face.

"We were waiting for you."

"Minsheng said that." I wondered where Daisy was

going with this conversation, but she didn't speak, her head to one side as if she was lost in a memory.

"Did my brother tell you why we signed up for the organization?" she asked eventually.

I shook my head but didn't interrupt.

"We both had a dream. A vision, if you like. I had it first, several nights in a row, and then he got it too. We realized they were the same when we both brought up the idea of moving to LA at pretty much the same time.

"You dreamed of LA?" I asked, not sure what this had to do with the organization or me.

"No. We dreamed of you, leading every single mythical on the planet into battle. From LA."

My mouth fell open. Every single mythical? How?

She chuckled when she saw my expression.

"I wasn't sure it was you at first. You look like her now, though. More elven than when we first met you, and you hold your head higher these days. You've got more confidence."

"Why didn't you say anything?"

"To be honest, we both thought it was Tuviel, not you. At least at first. The bronze dragon with her could easily have been Azargad. Of course, that was Zephyr."

"I'm not sure I want to lead all the mythicals in the world. Not into battle. That would mean there's a bigger threat out there than Jacobs."

There is. Zephyr let me know he'd been listening. *But Tuviel and Azargad didn't fight him on Earth, and he's been presumed dead for centuries.*

I blinked, not sure how to respond. Daisy stared at me, the dinner we were preparing momentarily forgotten.

"You're talking to Zephyr, aren't you?" she asked.

"Sort of. We barely have to talk to each other so much as just think in an unguarded way."

"Makes sense."

"But I still don't understand why everyone thinks I'm supposed to be riding into some big battle. Most of the human race likes us. It's not going to take long to get the few rogue agents to leave us alone." As the words came tumbling out, I knew my hopes were optimistic, but I couldn't help it. I wanted to believe that everything was going to be okay.

"The organization has always believed that one day the mythicals on this planet would have to defend everyone. They've never been very specific about what threat, but there are many in the organization who have had similar visions. They reached out to us when Minsheng and I started researching our vision of the future."

"And then they trained you?"

"Well, they trained Minsheng. He was always the better fighter and stronger dwarf."

I detected a hint of pain in Daisy's eyes and a catch in her voice as she spoke the last word, but before I could respond, others arrived. The conversation ended, but it left me with plenty to think about—and more than a few questions.

We'll talk about it when all this is over, Zephyr said in my head. *But I don't know a lot.*

CHAPTER TWENTY

Groaning as I stretched, I tried to get comfortable. I was sitting in a small space in the back of the armored vehicle, leaning against Zephyr, who was clearly just as uncomfortable.

The sun had begun to set, darkening our small world while Chris drove us toward the agents' base again. After using the stone to contact Ronan and explain the plan, we'd stopped at the new Sanctuary briefly, picking up Ronan, Seth, and another centaur who'd volunteered.

I'd been thinking about this for the last little while. The centaur had fought alongside Lorcan and us the previous night and decided to join us because of it, just as Seth had. Was this the sort of thing that had led to Daisy's vision?

There's nothing wrong with being a leader and inspiring others to fight for a cause, Zephyr pointed out.

No. It's just not what I used to imagine for my life.

You also didn't imagine yourself flying on a dragon.

Good point, I replied, smiling. Who did seriously believe that when they grew up they'd be a great dragon rider?

I shifted again, feeling Zephyr do the same.

Are we there yet? he thought a moment later.

This time I chuckled and felt him shake as he tried to suppress his own mirth. I considered passing the question on to Chris, but before I could, he took a sharp turn onto a bumpier road.

It answered Zephyr's question. We were almost there.

It only took a couple more minutes of bumping along to reach our destination, and Chris turned the engine off. Grateful to be able to stretch and aware Zephyr would need it even more, I flung open the back hatch and got out. Zephyr had to reverse, and then he turned, stretched his wings and sighed.

The others got out of two more vehicles, one of them similar to ours. We'd had to borrow both from the Sanctuary and promise to keep them safe. It wasn't easy for the mythicals to replace something like that without exposing themselves to danger.

From here, we would be traveling the last mile or so on foot through the wilderness. It wasn't ideal, but we wanted to sneak in. Well, most of us. Minsheng, Crawley, Erlan, and Newton got into our armored vehicle and prepared to set off. They were giving our other two groups a fifteen-minute head start to get to our positions.

Chris and our second centaur, Dyneira, were coming with us. Ronan was taking the final team, along with Seth, Daisy, and Justin, the only one of the three gnomes we'd rescued who was well enough to aid us.

The eight of us would travel most of the way together, and I led them out without any delay, Zephyr and I walking to set the pace. As we got close enough to the compound for the sentries to see us, Zephyr and I lifted into the air.

It was a heavily clouded night, and it got darker. We were coming in from the west, however, so that was to be expected.

We soon split into our two groups, mine heading to the northern portion of the base. Chris struggled to keep up until Dyneira pretty much grabbed him, lifted him off his feet, and stuck him on her back.

I stifled a laugh as Zephyr and I flew on. Dyneira ran, following the path we blazed through the sky.

When we had gone far enough around, Zephyr and I came in low again and flew more slowly. There was one sentry tower close enough to cause a problem, and it was clearly manned, the building lit from below.

Landing near a dark bush, Zephyr exhaled a small amount of gas and I took control of it. I lifted it up to the sentry tower, guided by Zephyr and his improved eyesight.

Left a bit, he said into my head. *No, the other left.*

I snorted as I moved it in the opposite direction and then I saw the shadow of the guard as he slumped over. It looked like the man might overbalance and fall out of the tower, so I gave him a blast of air to knock him back in. A moment later the sentry was neutralized.

Hurrying closer to the fence, and waving Dyneira over, I kept a look out for patrols. If any came, we'd have to act quickly and overpower them before they could warn anyone about us. The last thing we wanted to do was mobilize the entire base against us all at once.

We had a strong team, but based on the cars parked here alone, we were still vastly outnumbered and I didn't want to give them a chance to move their prisoner or hurt her before we attacked.

As we got to the fence I noticed movement. Immediately, Zephyr exhaled more gas, catching two agents on patrol full in the face as they came around a corner. Again I used my abilities to ensure their bodies fell into the shadows and didn't make too much noise as they hit the ground.

With a clear window, I blasted up into the air. Zephyr then did the same, flying over Dyneira before she could protest and picking her up while Chris was still on her back. By the time another minute had passed, we were all safely on the ground on the other side again.

We weren't far from where Zephyr and I had entered the first time. That was the quietest spot, and we'd instructed Ronan to take his group there. Daisy and Justin both had tranquilizer guns, but we weren't expecting them to enter the compound just yet. They were going to wait for a few minutes for Crawley to distract the agents on the other side.

While that was happening, our team hurried along the route I'd taken the first time, taking out a few more agents with gas. This time I didn't move them out of the base. I didn't want any on the outside when it came time for us to escape. The clearer our route back to safety the better.

With the extra help, it didn't take long to get to our first objective. Crouching at the corner of a building, Zephyr's head above me and Dyneira and Chris watching our rear, I waited for the distraction we needed.

As soon as Crawley appeared in the armored vehicle and demanded to be admitted, we were going to make our move, but now it was her turn to shine.

We'd either been faster this time or Minsheng, Crawley and their team were held up because we waited for what felt like ages for someone to turn up. Each minute ticked by in an agony of fear and doubt over what might have happened to them.

Eventually they appeared, however, and drew the attention of the agents near the entrance. The guards on the door of the main building barely glanced that way.

At least for now, they were going to treat it like a normal arrival.

It wasn't long before I heard Minsheng's raised voice declaring something unacceptable. Crawley had provided the information we needed for Minsheng to bluff his way in as Jacobs' superior, and a little hacking and improvisation from Erlan had given us identity passes. They wouldn't work on the doors, but they would get them inside the base and nearby.

The vehicle was finally let through, and I gave Dyneira the signal. She stopped in her tracks, her eyes flickering as she connected to Ronan and gave him the go-ahead to begin his part of the plan.

As Crawley opened the door of the now-parked vehicle, Erlan got to work with his magic and I saw Newton slip out, unnoticed, his color camouflaging him against the dirt. A fire started in a bush just inside the perimeter of the parking lot but far enough away that it didn't endanger our vehicle. It drew the guards' attention.

This time the guards near us were distracted, along

with several others who ran to get fire extinguishers and put the fire out. Before they could even begin fighting the flames, Erlan, still hidden inside the vehicle, started another fire on the other side of the parking lot, igniting a small barrel of some flammable liquid that exploded.

More guards went running, and there were shouts of possible mythical attacks. Almost all the guards rushed to the perimeter, and Crawley and Minsheng deliberately pulled back into their armored truck, joining them in aiming at the outside.

Adding to the charade, Minsheng fired and pointed at nothing but pretended it was something.

With everyone distracted, Zephyr exhaled some more gas for me. I lifted this ball into the air and split it in two, then brought it down over the guards at the door and knocked both out.

At the same time, Ronan and Dyneira kept up the stream of communication, and Seth set off another fire in the far corner of the base.

The guards were so distracted that some went running in that direction while I floated the two from the building onto the roof, stowing them out of the way. We then made our move.

Minsheng, Crawley, Erlan, and Newton turned on any guards they could see while I ran up to the doors and Chris worked on getting us inside.

Before he could hack the system, I used my air ability to haul over an agent I recognized. He'd scanned into the building the previous evening, so between Dyneira and me, we held him up and scanned his thumb again.

I grinned as the door clicked, and Chris pushed it open. I, Chris, and Dyneira donned gas masks, and Minsheng, Crawley, and Erlan pulled back to take the guard positions around the building, Newton scurrying up a sentry tower to keep an eye out for them.

Zephyr exhaled into the building a few times, and I blew the gas ahead of us. The dragon was too large to fit inside, but as soon as we were walking through a fog of paralyzing gas, Zephyr flew onto the roof and made his way to the air conditioning unit we'd spotted up there.

A moment later, he was exhaling large amounts of gas into the building in strategic areas. It took a while to filter through, but it gave me gas to work with.

So we could see, he stopped as soon as I told him the first puffs of white vapor were coming out of the vents. More continued to pour through the system and I worried we'd overloaded it, but eventually it settled in a layer above our heads that rolled about and started to spread.

I took control of it as we moved through the building. It wasn't long before I spotted two more downed agents, both paralyzed.

Taking a radio off the first, I listened to the chatter. It was still panicked, the expectation of the attack coming from outside, but there was one voice speaking loudly and clearly about the vapor in the main building.

"Secure the asset. Make sure no one goes in to speak to her or takes her anything. And look out for loose mythicals. Looks like some snuck out of that slum they call home before Mike and his team got there."

"Roger that," a voice replied.

So there were more of them in the building, but I couldn't be sure how many more.

I let the others know, and we kept going, Chris now on his own two feet with a tranquilizer gun in hand. I led the way, moving an unseen barrier of air in front of the three of us. We checked every room we went past, but most of them were empty.

Their uses varied from offices to storage closets and filing rooms. I trashed all of them as quickly as I could with my abilities, wishing I had one of the fire elves with me to set stuff alight. That would have to wait until we'd found Crawley's daughter.

As we reached a corner in the main corridor, I thought I heard a sound from ahead, so I held up a hand to slow my companions. Feeling for air movement, I tried to work out if anyone was on the other side.

I wasn't sure at first since the air was stirred by an aircon unit nearby, but eventually I noticed something acting strangely—an extra puff of air. Was someone standing there, exhaling? Tracing the movement, I felt it flow around a shape that in my head seemed humanoid. Then I noticed it doing the same around four more.

Two were crouched, but the other two stood, and I was pretty sure they had gas masks on. Despite that, I brought the gas clouds down toward the crouching pair or at least tried to. I couldn't see, so I had to try to work out what particles were Zephyr's gas by the way they resisted my control.

"What the hell!" I heard someone exclaim, then the shuffles of a bunch of people. I moved the gas even farther and was rewarded by the *thwump* of a person falling into a heap.

"Jim's down," the same voice said a moment later. I detected movement nearby, so I directed the cloud even closer and heard a muffled noise. The person tried to move away, getting even lower, but I followed, hoping I was controlling enough gas to knock them out, not just scare them.

A second slumping noise came around the corner, and I sensed the body go still. Two down, but the other two were clearly more cautious and wearing masks.

For a moment, no one moved or did anything. These two were not taking any chances. I held up two fingers, and I felt one of them lift an arm as well. They were about to attack.

I crouched as low as I could and pulled out the gun I carried. This was enough of a signal for my two companions.

The second the two men came around the corner, Chris and Dyneira fired and hit them with tranq darts, feathers sticking out of their chests as they tried to return fire.

Bullets sprayed outward as I blasted air at them to knock them off-target. Most went high anyway, the agents passing out before they could aim.

I sighed as the corridor went quiet. I'd hoped to avoid gunfire if possible. The other agents in the building were going to know we were coming now. As if confirming my thought, the radio in my ear crackled to life again.

"Gunfire down the east corridor. Green team moving to intercept," a voice I'd not heard yet said.

"More incoming," I whispered to my companions,

wondering just how many agents were inside this building. Color-coded teams meant there were many, and they were keeping their heads better than most. I had a feeling they were better trained and smarter.

Feeling tense, I did the only thing I could: I led my team on.

CHAPTER TWENTY-ONE

As time ticked by and we went deeper into the building, I grew tenser. It didn't help that I was apart from Zephyr. I never liked it, and in the depths of a battle, it was even worse.

We'd passed a few more rooms, opening the doors more cautiously now that I knew people were coming our way. Again we found rooms that weren't occupied, but I didn't bother trashing any of these. We couldn't afford the noise it would make.

Before we could go much farther, a sound from behind startled all of us and made us whirl around. Crawley appeared, along with Erlan and Newton, both people wearing gas masks. I frowned. They were supposed to be outside, not in here.

"We heard gunfire," Crawley said quietly, her pistol clutched in one hand but not aimed upward.

Newton sat on Erlan's shoulder despite being closer to the gas, but the young elf looked ready for battle and heat radiated off him. Before I could send them back, I felt movement in the air deeper in the building.

I put a finger to my lips before turning again and trying to get an idea of where the agents were.

More gas, Zephyr, I said in my head, hoping he was listening and the vapor would come through quickly.

It was starting to dissipate, and not being able to see gave me an advantage over everyone else when I could feel them moving through the air with my abilities. It made it harder on those with me, but I could keep them safe, and I was beginning to suspect the salamanders were immune to Zephyr's gas.

On it, he replied a moment later, relief washing through me that he was okay and able to respond.

Concentrating, I took a step forward and another. Someone was ahead, but they weren't moving very fast, almost as if they were inching this way. I couldn't tell if there were more people or just one yet.

Everyone in the group had a weapon raised, and even Erlan had lifted his hand as if he might chuck a fireball at something at any moment.

I made the barrier guarding us thicker and took control of some gas as I felt for more movement. With the slow, steady pace of the person or group ahead, I was struggling to work out if they were friend or foe, but eventually I saw the toe tip of a boot as someone came to the edge of an open doorway. Dyneira shot without hesitating.

There was a dull grunt, and the man fell over. I used an air blast to knock him toward us and into the corridor. A scientist wearing a white lab coat fell to the floor. We got closer, everyone trying to be silent.

I crouched to look around the doorway and saw some kind of lab. On one of the nearby tables was an orb. It had patches of tape on it, holding wires in place, and it was hooked up to several machines. It looked to be active.

After ripping off the wires, I stuffed the orb into my bag, grateful it wasn't a strong enough light to glow through.

"We need to destroy everything in this room," I said. Whatever they were doing with orbs, I intended to make it hard for them to progress any further. Hopefully, they'd have no other versions of this equipment stored elsewhere.

"We should probably check that there's no backups of this data," Erlan replied in a whisper.

"Can you do that?"

"I can give it a try, but it will take me a few minutes."

Chris came up to Erlan as he sat by one of the nearby computers and started typing.

"I'll keep an eye on our friends here and help destroy what's needed when the time comes," Chris said, pulling the scientist's body back into the room to hide the evidence.

"Close the door after us," I replied. "And get out and join the others as soon as you're done."

"Got it, boss," Chris replied. "Don't worry about us."

I was concerned we'd need Chris' skills, but he was the most logical person to leave with Erlan. Whatever the agents were up to in the lab, it didn't bode well, and the pair of them working together were more likely to put a stop to it and remove all the info the agents already had.

My main mission was getting Crawley's daughter back, however, and I was pretty sure Crawley wasn't going to wait much longer before she took matters into her own hands.

I could only hope any agents ahead were in small groups since we were down to three again.

Zephyr's breath weapon lay thick over the top third of the corridor, so I asked him to stop again.

Good, because I was beginning to feel a little lightheaded. You owe me a serious amount of pizza.

As long as I can eat plenty too.

See if you can find someone's credit card. Jacobs' would be best," Zephyr suggested.

I grinned but didn't respond. There was nothing like Zephyr's sense of humor to make me feel more relaxed. I hadn't noticed how tense I was until we finished our little conversation.

Not much later, I felt more movement up ahead. This time, there were clearly several of them, but they were also being cautious.

I could feel them coming through what seemed to be open doorways, pausing, almost as if they were checking rooms and then coming this way.

Holding up my hands again, I paused by a couple of open side rooms and crouched just inside one of them. Crawley joined me, and Dyneira moved to the opposite side. It was harder for her to crouch, so she hung back, watching me instead.

Coming down the corridor ahead were four men. I used a blast of air to pull their legs out from under them before they could spot us. Crawley and then Dyneira stepped out and shot at the prone forms.

All four were wearing bulletproof vests and took hits

with no effect. I winced at the bruises they were likely to have before they hunkered down and found doorways of their own.

With all of us low, it was a strange battle, my air blasts sending bullets off course and buying time for our people to shoot. These men knew what they were doing, however, and the opportunities to retaliate were few.

After several back-and-forth volleys, Crawley ducked back in and started reloading her pistol.

"Can you get us through somehow?" she asked as another bullet just missed Dyneira. I frowned. What could I do in this situation? The agents were wearing gas masks and Kevlar.

I tried to think of anything that might give us an advantage, but there was only one trick that might work, and I wasn't amazing at it yet.

Looking out into the corridor, I started separating out the hotter and colder air and pulling it around. A moment later, I was twirling it and forcing it to go faster and faster.

It was a difficult process, and I couldn't concentrate on anything else at the same time. That gave the soldiers free rein to try to get closer, but I tried to put that out of my mind.

Letting the pressure of the situation make me anxious would make me more likely to fail. Slowly, a translucent tornado started to form, picking up dust and whirling it around. It also picked up a few spent bullets and other debris until it was clearly the beginnings of an indoor twister.

I urged it toward the soldiers and heard exclamations. While I moved it, I continued to try to make it more powerful, but just keeping it going was making it taxing until I reached an aircon vent high up on the corridor wall. The blast of cold air from the top fueled the temperature difference it needed, and it whipped around even faster.

The swirling mass made a whistling noise as it spun and sucked in even more debris, beginning to grow less translucent. Still it kept coming at the soldiers, but I needed to look out of the room I was in to keep it going.

It exposed me to the men, but they were so shocked by what they were seeing that all their attention was on the twister. Beside me, Crawley also leaned out, and she took a shot. The first men went down, dead.

I tried not to gasp or lose concentration at the violence. I'd known she was shooting real bullets and why. These people had taken her daughter, but I wasn't happy about killing.

The gunshot snapped the men out of their freeze, and they aimed at us again. I had to duck back inside a room as a bullet clipped the wall not far from where my head had been.

It made it harder to control the twister, but I sent it on and was rewarded with strange grunts and whimpers when it reached the soldiers.

Looking out once more, I saw that it had surrounded the nearest man and was pelting him with spent bullets, dust, and all sorts of other stuff. The twister had also sucked in a fair amount of Zephyr's vapor, and the debris caused small scratches that made it easier for the vapor to get into his skin. He soon slumped to the floor.

Grinning, I moved my twister on. It was losing speed,

but we'd reduced the four-man team to two, and those odds made me feel a lot better.

The next man quickly succumbed as well, but the final one tried to run.

I let go of the air in the tornado briefly to use a blast to knock the soldier over. He dropped his gun, and I lifted it and smacked him over the head with it.

All four agents were finally neutralized.

"Everyone all right?" I asked as I stood again and deliberately slowed and dissipated the twister.

"If we can find Emily, I will be," Crawley replied, moving to the men. She started pulling ammo packs off the nearest agent and also grabbed a radio and plugged it into her ear.

"It's awfully quiet down there, Jace. Report?" the radio said as Dyneira and I hurried to catch up with Crawley, who was tightening zip ties around the wrists and ankles of the men and dragging them into a storage closet.

"Should we respond?" I asked Crawley when the same voice repeated his message.

"No. We can't fool them, and they're already suspicious. We've just got to do our thing as quickly as we can."

I nodded and resumed our crouched infiltration of the building.

The next door led to some stairs that went upward. It also opened to another part of the building that was in darkness.

"Stay here and watch the stairs," Crawley said. "I'll quickly check these rooms, but I suspect they're all empty as well."

She didn't wait for a response and that gave me no

choice, but I wasn't happy about taking orders from her. This was my mission to command, even if I could appreciate her situation. Not only was she used to giving the instructions, but this was about her daughter.

I also knew she had more experience in this sort of setting. For all I knew, she might have even been here before. It kept me quiet and accepting of her command.

Thankfully it didn't take Crawley long and she was soon back by my side. Before she could even attempt to take the lead, I made my way upward. It was possibly petty of me, but it was also sensible. I had a barrier against bullets. I might have been getting tired, but I was still our best attacker and defender.

On the floor above, the air was even thicker with gas, and it had settled at a lower position. There was no way to head underneath it anymore. We were going to have to go in and make sure we weren't exposed to it for too long.

The radio had been quiet, either because there wasn't anyone left to talk to or they'd realized we could probably listen in by now, so all we could do was keep going and hope we were near the end of our mission.

I paused at the exit to another corridor, lowering myself to see both ways. I could just make out a set of feet as someone patrolled, and then they bent their knees, clearly about to crouch. I pulled back into the stairwell and motioned to Crawley and Dyneira with my hand to let them know what I'd seen.

Slowly, footsteps approached, and we pulled farther and farther back. As the guard was about to appear, I shot a tranquilizer dart at the nearest leg. Since it was only a couple of feet away, I easily hit my target. A moment later the man slumped, probably having no idea what had hit him.

Crawley grabbed an arm and pulled him into the stairwell. It wasn't an ideal place to leave the unconscious man, but it would have to do. A lone guard was a surprise, but possibly it was a sign that we'd significantly reduced their numbers.

How's it going? Zephyr asked. *The others out here are getting antsy. Worried it's taking too long.*

There's been a lot of people in here, but I think we're close, I replied as I hurried onward. There was a slight indent in the corridor ahead, and I could see more feet.

Crawley reached for my arm and pulled me back. She then put a finger to her lips.

I tried to shake my head to tell her not to try whatever she was thinking of, but she ignored me, straightened up, and checked that her identity pin was in place. Then she strode up to the men.

"We're still trying to locate the infiltrators, and they've been listening to the comms. Is the prisoner secure?" she asked loud enough that I could hear. Inch by inch, I continued to move closer, shielded by the vapor and the wall for now.

"She's been making a fuss. Scared by this gas, no doubt," one of the men replied. "But we'll teach her a lesson when the area is secure again. Not going to defy Jacobs' commands and open this thing until we know there's no one here to get her out."

"Good. I'll head back to Jace now. They think they've almost got the bastards cornered."

"Glad to hear it."

I smiled at how Crawley had fooled the men. A moment later she lifted her gun, and I knew this was her moment. I blasted upright and around the corner, using extra air to make me faster, and shot the nearest guard in the leg. He tried to lift his gun, so I hit it with a blast of air to push it down.

It almost didn't work since my powers were drained, but the man collapsed before he could get a shot off. Beside me, Crawley stood over another dying agent.

"You should never have laid a finger on my daughter," Crawley said to the man as he bled out.

I gulped, hearing the fury in the mother's voice and seeing the understanding as it filled the man's eyes.

Turning to the door, I tried to work out how to open it, but there wasn't anything obvious.

"Stand back and prepare to shoot anyone who hears this and comes running," Dyneira said before pulling back across the corridor and then lashing out at the door handle with her powerful hooves.

On the third loud kick, the door burst open, revealing a small but relatively comfortable cell. There wasn't as much gas in the room, although a feeble-looking aircon unit sat on the right-hand wall, but there was some. More poured in as the woman inside got off the bed.

"Mom!" She raced over to Crawley, and the two embraced before Crawley handed her a gas mask.

"We shouldn't stick around," I said, hating to interrupt. "Gather anything that's yours, and we'll get you both some-where safer."

The woman finally looked my way. She was a couple of inches taller than her mother but sported the same brown hair. The daughter's was a little longer, and two ever-so-slightly pointed ears poked out from underneath it.

"I've got nothing to take," she replied calmly.

As she looked at her mother again, I noticed a yellowing bruise on the side of her cheek just below the eye. There were a few more on her arms. At some point, she'd taken a beating.

"Come on, then," I said. "Let's get out of here and go home."

CHAPTER TWENTY-TWO

It didn't take us long to get Crawley and her daughter back down to the next level, then we were hurrying back the way we'd come.

Zephyr's vapor had started to clear, so we could jog along almost upright. I didn't get him to add any more. There was a good chance we'd neutralized anyone else in the building.

Despite that, I tried to feel ahead for movement. I was using up my energy on magic, so I grabbed a granola bar and ate it with one hand, my gun ready in the other. I followed it with a second and a third, the final one getting me looks when I stuffed it down my throat as quickly as the first two.

"Magic makes me hungry," I said when I could take the questioning looks from Crawley and her daughter no longer.

"You're one of them?" Emily asked, her eyes lighting up and getting wider.

"I'm part-elf just like you, if that's what you mean."

"I'm part what?" she exclaimed, her voice shrill.

"You don't know?" I blinked as Crawley gave me a look. It seemed I'd just gotten Mommy into trouble. Or at least given her some explaining to do.

"We should keep going," I added and picked up the pace again.

It wasn't long before I could feel movement again, but it was coming from inside the lab and so was probably Chris and Erlan.

I knocked on the door and called their names.

"Almost done," Chris replied before opening the door and admitting us.

Erlan was standing over a pile of computer pieces and the desks sported hollowed-out husks of former machines. Wires and other components were strewn everywhere.

Before our eyes, Erlan and Newton started a fire among the components, adding bits of wooden furniture from around the room to help it burn.

As soon as the blaze was established, I ushered them out of the room and floated the guy in the lab coat with us, then led the team back to the front door. There were no challenges, but just in case, Dyneira and Chris brought up the rear and made sure our growing team didn't get ambushed from behind.

We were only a couple of hundred meters from the front door when I heard shooting and shouts coming from outside. All of us broke into a run, heading for the sounds of danger.

What's happening? I asked Zephyr, sensing him launching upward and get farther away from me.

More agents. They've come from somewhere else, like they were coming back. Lots more agents.

Shitsticks.

Before Zephyr could tell me anything else, I passed on the information to the team. They needed to know we were walking into a seriously hostile situation.

I reached the door first, finding Minsheng, Seth, and Justin crouched near it. All three of them were shooting projectiles of some kind at agents who had pulled up in cars and similarly armored vehicles.

At least fifty agents poured out of them, and all of them firing at my friends.

"We're screwed," Emily said as she caught sight of what we were up against. I wasn't sure she was wrong. The last time we'd fought this many agents at once, I'd been fresh, and we'd had crowds to help us. The time before that, we'd had traps and a maze.

This time we were in the open, and I'd already taxed my abilities significantly.

Agent Crawley looked at me, and I knew she expected me to handle it. Whatever happened next, someone needed to take some heat off this door so my people could get to our bulletproof vehicle. There was a chance everyone but Zephyr and I could get in and get away while my dragon and I drew the agent fire and caused havoc.

I removed the Kevlar vest from one of the door guards and pulled it on, strapping it as best I could. It was a little too big, but it would have to do.

"Everyone pull inside a bit," I said. "I'm going to need some clearance, and I'm going to create quite a backblast."

Minsheng looked at me with worried eyes. Big ideas

and displays of power were why I was here, however, and he knew better than to try to talk me out of anything.

They all did as I asked by the time I was wearing the Kevlar and had gotten another good look outside.

"When you get the opportunity, make for the truck and get out of here. Don't worry about Zephyr and me. We'll fly after you as soon as we can."

"Got it," Chris replied for the group.

"Oh, and Erlan, Seth?" I asked, looking at the two other elves.

"Yes, boss?" Erlan replied.

"Burn this place to the ground."

Erlan grinned, and Seth looked away from the agents outside for a moment to shoot me a more-than-happy look at the prospect.

Without another backward look, I summoned all the control I could and built the pressure of air around me until I made my own ears pop. Then I blasted downward and back from my hands and feet.

I shot out of the doorway like a rocket, heading up and toward Zephyr as he flew over. We came together, gunfire following me until he caught me and wheeled away with both of us.

With dismay, I noticed a fresh tear in his right wing. He'd been shot, and while his hide could withstand the bullets, his wings struggled. It would heal in time. Small tears did, but too many would make it far harder for him to fly.

We need to distract them, I said. *You up for it?*

Always. Let's thin the herd a bit first, shall we? Gas a few?

A bunch look like they're pulling on gas masks. We'd best make it quick.

Already on it. His body shifted, preparing to expel the paralyzing fumes. I reached for the particles to control the gas as it came out of him and propelled it down and forward. At the same time, I formed a thick barrier of air underneath us to slow any bullets that came toward his wings while we flew overhead.

Several agents went down, enveloped in gas they couldn't help but breathe, but plenty had gotten the masks on in time.

That didn't stop me from reaching back as we finished a sweep and blasting air at any weapons that had been put down or were held in awkward grips while their owners hastily tried to strap on their gas masks.

Guns and ammo packs went skittering across the parking lot and I blasted them again, sending them toward my friends as backup weapons. Some of the weaponless agents quickly took more off paralyzed comrades near them, but a few were left weaponless. Either way, our maneuver bought a reprieve for the mythicals to run for the back of the armored truck.

Come around the back this time, I suggested. Seth had lit a few bushes on that side, and now that I knew Zephyr's gas was flammable, it gave me an idea.

He happily obliged, clearly catching on to what I was suggesting. I grinned since I had little to do this time but protect us with my air barrier. We flew in really low from behind.

The agents scrambled to turn, but that meant they got a faceful as Zephyr exhaled. As the vapor crossed the naked flames, it became a giant ball of rolling fire, and I blasted it even farther, engulfing the middle section of agents.

Screams as much of fear as pain reached my ears, and then we were flying above the agents while banking. Again I took the opportunity to steal what weapons I could and blast the agents with air.

The agents on the left were more organized and held together better, putting out the fires on their clothes. Those who could returned fire.

Zephyr banked right and pulled up but not before another few bullets got through and hit his underside. I heard him grunt and knew he'd have a few more bruises. I glanced at his wings to see he had a couple more small holes as well.

We'd thinned the crowd to two-thirds of their forces, but we couldn't easily repeat our moves. I was panting and shaking, my abilities almost spent, and it had come at the price of a considerable number of bullets hitting Zephyr on both flybys.

Remind me to work out how we can armor you without slowing you down, I said as we came back around, too far away for any of the agents to be bothering to shoot at us anymore.

Most of our friends were now in the truck, Daisy in the driver's seat and Minsheng and Agent Crawley each shooting from a side window. Ronan was in the back too, shooting around the side with Justin. Emily was also safe, holding out her arms to help others up beside her.

Erlan, Seth, and Dyneira were still by the building, hurling fire in all directions, and Chris was nowhere to be seen.

We needed to distract our attackers a little more. While we banked around the back, I grabbed another granola bar and ate it as quickly as I could, looking for weak targets and mulling ideas.

I was just going to suggest we'd need to repeat our last attack when one of the buildings exploded. Fire went everywhere, and parts of the building flew into the air.

I used my powers to keep it off my friends, funneling the flying chunks of concrete and metal through the gap between the truck and the main building and straight at the agents. A large section of twisted metal landed on a car, taking out the shield the agents had been using, and I gave it another blast to move it even farther.

This tactic downed another six agents between falling debris and weapons fire. That left a little over half of them. I chowed down on another granola bar; I was sick of the flavor, but I needed as much energy as my body could metabolize.

Somehow I needed to reduce the numbers further or the truck wasn't going to get through.

Get back to Seth and Erlan, Zephyr said into my head. I started to object. *Get them to make a fire in the end agent vehicles. I'll fly by and lay more gas across them. You can then make a barrier and get everyone else to safety.*

I still didn't like the idea, but he had a point, and it was the safest way to get the other three to the truck. They'd not been able to run because the agents were now dividing their attention. They must have worked out what we were trying to do.

While Zephyr was still a long way away from the agents, I blasted off his back and over the roof of the front building. I drew fire, but I blasted air in that direction and redirected most of the bullets. The rest managed to miss me.

As I landed, I blasted even more air at the agents and darted into the building again. Within seconds, I'd passed on Zephyr's idea. Bullets whizzed toward us, but Dyneira and I did our best to return fire and keep the agents from getting good shots while Seth and Erlan concentrated.

Zephyr flew by as both cars exploded.

"Run," I shouted, forming a barrier like a large oval shield as best I could.

Seth was the first to get moving, then Dyneira grabbed Erlan's arm and hurried the young elf along. I ran behind and to one side, half-grateful most of the agents concentrated on me and half-terrified.

Thankfully, Zephyr's flyby had created a lot more fire, and those had started mini-fires. The area the agents were in had to be sweltering hot, if nothing else. Bullets ricocheted and bounced around, however, the firepower increasing as the agents recovered.

Seth was safe first, but Dyneira took a bullet to the flank as she shoved Erlan up, the horse part of her body exposed. A moment later, my shield phased out, my abilities fully drained. I immediately took a bullet to the chest, and it knocked me off my feet.

I groaned in pain, wondering if I was dying. Zephyr landed over me, growling and roaring, his head down under the onslaught of bullets. They pinged off his scales, and he kept his wings tucked in tight behind his large shoulders.

I heard the squeal of truck tires and the noise changed, sounding like bullets pinging off metal.

Aella? Zephyr's panicked voice sounded in my head. It made me jump, reminding me of the pain I felt, but also that I was still very much alive. I exhaled and pushed up off the asphalt with nothing but my normal strength.

I'm alive, I replied, looking at the vest I wore. It had saved my life, but I was going to have some pretty big bruises. Not only where the bullet struck, but where I hit the ground after.

Get behind me and climb up my back far enough to hold on, Zephyr said, his voice commanding in a way I'd never heard before. He was pissed off—*so* pissed off.

I had a feeling the agents were going to regret what they'd just done, but Zephyr wasn't the only one who was angry.

"She's safe!" I heard Erlan yell, although I wasn't sure how he knew until I saw him scoop Newton up off the ground behind the truck. The fire salamander had rushed to help me too.

I was so touched that everyone had put themselves in danger to protect me that I almost cried, but we still had a battle to finish, and there were clearly still plenty of agents with weapons.

I heard rather than saw the truck rev and head toward the agents' line of cars.

Fear washed through me, both for the agents and my friends. There was no knowing how a collision would change the situation, but Daisy clearly felt confident.

They'd better all be strapped in tight, I told Zephyr since I couldn't tell anyone else at this point.

I'm sure they are, but I hope you're focused on holding on.

As well as I can.

I gripped Zephyr's back tightly and latched onto a couple of the thorny spines on this part of his torso. They'd made his back interesting to climb, but they were going to help me stay put while I recuperated in more ways than one.

While the truck was still in front and distracting the agents for us, he leaped into the air before unfurling his wings and taking flight. We soared over the battle as the truck hit the first two cars.

I could have sworn one of them exploded before the truck hit it, and the other was broken from the falling debris earlier. The agents scattered as Zephyr dived around to one side of the truck instead of going high.

He stretched in a strange way, and I heard the crunch of more metal.

Did you just pick up a car? I asked.

No, he replied. *Two cars. I'm going...bowling, I think you call it.*

A moment later, I heard the crunches of the two flying projectiles as they hit the ground and then repeated crunches followed by yells and screams as agents were hit by the rolling cars.

As Zephyr wheeled around to come back again, I looked at the carnage and devastation. Only a few agents were left standing. Everyone else was injured, unconscious, or worse.

I couldn't believe the destruction we'd caused between us all. Our truck was also totaled however. There was steam coming out of the engine, and the thing refused to start again.

Land, I told Zephyr as the remaining agents lifted their hands and dropped their guns. Minsheng and Crawley jumped out of our truck, still aiming guns and encouraging the four men and one woman left standing to come closer together and wait where they could be seen.

The second Zephyr was on solid ground, I got down and pulled my weapon again. I only had darts, but they were effective enough.

"Any one of you, Mike, by any chance?" I asked.

One of the agents stepped forward, his hands behind his head.

"That would be me."

I walked up to him, holding my gun out in front of me.

"You're going to nod or shake your head to a few yes-or-no questions I want answers to. If I think you're lying at any point or you give me excuses and shit I don't want to hear, I'm going to shoot you and hand you over to Zephyr here. He's hungry and pissed about being shot at. You understand?"

Mike nodded as he gulped and glanced at the dragon towering over everyone.

Zephyr let out a roar to add to the drama and threat.

"Were you trying to attack the Sanctuary tonight?"

A nod. At least he'd started truthfully. He couldn't know I already knew the answer to that question.

"I guess you didn't find it."

Now a shake. It hadn't been a question, but again, it was a truthful answer. I thought for a moment.

"Did Jacobs send you?"

Another nod.

"To kill them?"

Shake.

"Take them alive?"

"Where possible," he replied. "But—"

I lifted my gun again.

"Unless it's useful information or answers my question, I don't want to hear your buts."

Mike shut his mouth with an audible snap.

"Did you find any mythicals at all?"

There was a hesitation before he shook his head. I studied him.

"Out with it. What else happened?"

Mike didn't say anything.

"Spit it out or I hand you over to the dragon," I said, lowering my voice and enunciating every word extra clearly.

"We split the group. Knew the Sanctuary was moving out. A bunch went off with another orb to look for the new position and see if we could ambush them on the way somewhere or before they've fully set up their defenses."

"How long ago?"

"Right before we came back and found you. About an hour. You'll never catch them."

I growled and shot without hesitation.

Mike's eyes went wide, then he passed out. I looked at the other four.

"You'd better start running, but don't even think about taking anything with you," I said to them as the rest of my friends got out of the broken truck.

I looked at them, knowing the mythicals from the Sanctuary had heard enough to understand the place was in danger.

"Find whatever vehicles still run. We'll borrow whatever looks strongest. Then Erlan, Seth, you know what to do."

Without another word, I got onto Zephyr's back again, and he took off. We had more agents to stop.

CHAPTER TWENTY-THREE

To say we were tired was an understatement, but there was no way we were stopping.

We'd eaten the rest of the snacks I had between us, and we'd even stopped at an all-night store we'd seen along the way to grab more food and drink, but only for the briefest moment possible.

I could tell Zephyr hurt, but the Sanctuary didn't know they had trouble coming their way, and we'd left stragglers on the road between the Sanctuary's two positions. They could easily be caught on the way or lead the agents right to the new position.

When they'd begun the move, they might have said they'd done it because the agents had discovered them without my interference, but I'd also told them I'd protect them, and they'd picked one of the locations I'd recommended.

If something happened to them now, I knew they'd blame me. More importantly, *I'd* blame me.

We'd been flying for another hour and weren't far from

the new location we'd suggested to the Sanctuary when Zephyr swooped a little lower.

I think I see them, he said, his voice deep and rumbling in my head, but also tired. Thankfully, riding on his back had given me a little energy.

Somewhere behind us were Minsheng and the others, all riding in whatever they could find. I hadn't waited to see what, but I'd connected with Ronan briefly while we'd stopped. He'd let me know they weren't far behind, although we could fly faster and take a direct route. He'd also promised to try to contact Lorcan and tell him what might be coming.

We flew closer, the night shielding us from view, but we were still wary. It was clearly a large convoy of cars, all following a lead vehicle. I also spotted two personnel transport vehicles and a couple of armored trucks that looked like they could take a serious amount of firepower, like the one we'd borrowed.

It wasn't a slow-moving convoy, either.

How far do you think we are from the Sanctuary? I asked Zephyr. The dragon was far better with distances than I was.

I'm not sure. After we left, I spent a lot of time in a truck that wasn't big enough.

Good point.

And you still owe me pizza.

I've not found a credit card to swipe from someone yet. But rest assured, we'll get pizza.

Just as long as it's not been forgotten.

Pizza will never be forgotten, I replied, unable to take my eyes off the array of cars we were trailing.

We needed to do something to slow them down, but I wasn't sure what.

Zephyr suddenly put on more speed and powered ahead of the cars. When we were a reasonable distance ahead of them, he slowed, came around, and then dropped, swooping over the front car and narrowly missing the road.

All four of the leading cars swerved off the road, and the ones behind screeched to a halt.

I laughed as Zephyr soared back up and peeled off to one side. We'd be hard to spot but not impossible, so it was important that we kept out of gun range most of the time.

The men opened and shut car doors as they conversed and whoever was in charge decided what he wanted to do. After a few minutes where some of them looked around as if they were trying to find us in the sky, they got back into their cars.

By the time they were up to speed, I estimated we'd bought about five minutes of catch-up time for our team. It wasn't a massive amount, but in a battle, it could make a world of difference.

Flying after them again, I considered what else might encourage the cars to slow or make our battle with them easier when the time came.

Trail behind them near the side of the road, I asked Zephyr as an idea popped into my head. He slid behind the row of cars and gently came down lower.

In the dark and flying along, it wasn't easy to see what I was looking for, but I spotted several bits of stone and debris eventually and used my abilities to pick them up.

When I had them in the air with us, I brought them

over to me. They were a couple of flattish flints, a broken piece of metal, and an old glass bottle shard. Being particularly careful with the latter, I considered the best use of the four projectiles.

Can you get us closer to the second truck? I asked Zephyr. *The one that probably has loads of people in?*

I'll try.

Zephyr put in more effort again, speeding up, but he also came in a little higher, making it harder for the agents in the cars below and behind to notice us.

From my perch on his back, I focused on the back left wheel of the truck and selected one of the stones. The glass was sharper, but I'd never done this before, and I didn't want to waste my best shot on my first attempt.

I imagined a channel of air between me and the truck wheel and sent the stone zipping along it as hard as I could. It struck the wheel but not hard enough to do anything more than bounce off and roll harmlessly away.

Exhaling to try to calm myself, I narrowed the air beam for a faster passage and tried again with the next flint. This one came out of the beam near the end, my control not quite good enough.

It hit the back of the truck instead and ricocheted into the windshield of the car behind. The glass shattered, covering the agents inside and making them stop.

That hadn't been the goal, but given that the car had at least two agents inside, it was a result I was happy to accept. I could always get more rocks if my tire-puncture idea proved useless.

I hesitated over my next weapon. The glass or the broken metal?

Eventually I decided to try to trust myself. This time, I went for a channel between the size of the last two and focused on the tire. I hurled the glass before I could second-guess myself.

There was a bang as it hit the back tire and decimated it. The truck swerved, and the driver clearly struggled to correct the course. I was rewarded with the sight of the truck pulling over as the entire convoy came to a halt again.

Good shot, Zephyr said as he rose and banked away from the road so we could watch from a safe distance.

I'd hoped the truck would be left behind on its own like the car with the shattered windshield, but we didn't get lucky that way. The agents and what looked like some soldiers got out of the back, and all of them helped replace the blown tire. I frowned. That wasn't what I'd hoped for.

With so many helpers and what was clearly plenty of supplies, the tire was changed in fifteen minutes, then the convoy got on the road again.

We bought more time for our friends to catch up and the Sanctuary to prepare, Zephyr reminded me as I growled from his back.

I know.

Time was better than nothing, but I wasn't managing to even the odds very well. Slowly, I calmed down again, and Zephyr flew us after the agents.

He'd benefitted from the rest as well, but we were going to have to make a move soon or they were going to pinpoint the Sanctuary for the third time since I'd begun visiting it.

I grabbed more rocks and debris as we lifted into the air

again. Maybe I could try taking out several tires at once. Make it too difficult for them to replace them all. But I had a feeling it was going to be my last attempt either way. The agents would know this was an attack when it happened again.

I took several deep breaths and steadied myself on Zephyr as I selected the best-looking projectiles from the stuff I'd swept up with my powers.

A moment later, I was creating five channels at once, the exertion making my head ache. I hurled all five at the two trucks and an armored vehicle, this time on the right-hand side of the convoy.

All five hit, but only four tires blew out. One tire on the back truck held up, the stone perhaps not as sharp, but the front truck swerved and the driver lost control. It careened off the road with a screech.

The armored tank-like vehicle didn't react to having a blown-out tire, having another behind it on the same side of the axle, but once again, the convoy halted. This time the soldiers fanned out, forming a protective ring.

Just as I'd suspected, they'd figured out they were under attack. This time Zephyr landed a little farther away in a clearing to one side of the road. We couldn't see the convoy as well, but we could see enough to know they were having a conversation this time instead of just changing the tires.

I've got an idea, Zephyr said. *Can you shield any noise we make?*

Of course, I replied, slipping off his back as he crept into the forest.

It wasn't easy to move quietly among trees when Zephyr was so big, but he squeezed through the larger gaps and found his way to a section of the forest that was closer to the soldiers but in such darkness there was no way they would spot us.

With very little warning, Zephyr exhaled toward the soldiers, turning his head as he did so the vapor formed in an arc. The wind blew gently through the trees and pushing the gas ahead of it. I grinned, wondering if the soldiers would notice before it hit them.

To maximize the effect, I formed an air barrier just out of sight of the enemy and let the gas build into a fog-like cloud of roiling fumes. Zephyr chuckled as it grew bigger, and when the soldiers looked like they were about to move out again, I not only let it go but blew it gently toward them.

There was so much that even with me blowing air at it, it stayed in a cloud and rolled over the soldiers and agents. Some of the men with experience of Zephyr's paralyzing gas were quick to grab gas masks and pull them on, but many were too slow or oblivious to the danger before it was too late.

Zephyr chuckled, the sound infectious enough to have me doing it as well.

Our gassing of the agents caused chaos, and Zephyr and I came together and got back into the air to survey the effects. We'd barely moved when the soldiers wearing gas masks opened fire, shooting into the forest where we'd been moments before.

I exhaled with relief that we'd thought to move, not sure we'd both still be alive if we hadn't. There were a lot of bullets, and this unit of men was using more aggressive weaponry, assault rifles and guns with stands that rattled through huge belts of ammo.

Probably a good time to hang back where they can't see us, I said to Zephyr, but he didn't need the encouragement to lift us up and away, hiding us under a large cloud.

While we were up there, I spotted the vehicles our team had taken from the agents. They consisted of another of the armored tank-like vehicles and two of the agents' cars.

I had no way of warning them that significant danger was ahead without revealing ourselves, but Zephyr flew toward them without me needing to ask.

We could only watch as they came closer.

Of course, the agents they were approaching had no idea it was my team in the vehicles coming up the road. It probably looked like reinforcements at the exact moment they needed them.

We should prepare to attack. Zephyr's deep voice sounded in my head, and he veered around the convoy to the head. I could see the merit in his tactic and understood what he was planning as soon as he conceived of doing it, as if the bond between us was now strong enough that feelings and desires were passing between us as well as thoughts.

Still, we were likely to come under a lot of fire, and I was really tired.

I'm scared, I admitted a moment later.

Me too. I don't think it would be right not to be scared, but we can't let this many soldiers get to the Sanctuary. They'll wipe out almost every mythical on this continent in one fell swoop.

Thinking about what might happen to our friends at the Sanctuary reminded me I had to fight, fear or not, and I had to give it everything. I wasn't alone, and our ancestors had fought all sorts of dangers in the past. I just had to hope and keep trying.

But I was also aware that I needed to use my powers wisely. I wasn't powerful enough to control the air all day every day and not be broken partway through. I had to help turn the tide of this battle in clever ways, while preserving enough energy to protect Zephyr and me from bullets.

That meant looking for weaknesses in the soldiers' defenses. While Zephyr flew us around beneath the clouds, I tried to do just this.

The vapor was clearing and revealing that we'd already taken out about half the soldiers and some of the agents. Everyone left standing was wearing a gas mask so Zephyr couldn't do any more damage that way, but we still had cards to play, and they didn't know where we were or how many people they were now up against.

With the trucks almost fixed thanks to a seeming abundance of spare tires, we weren't going to have long to make our move, but Minsheng, Daisy, and Chris almost had their vehicles pulled up behind.

The fireworks were about to begin.

CHAPTER TWENTY-FOUR

For a moment it looked like Daisy was going to pretend to be an ally, even when the soldiers came up to her, but the officer approaching to have a conversation and no doubt ask for ID took a dart to the neck a few seconds later.

The commotion this caused was perfect as it rippled outward. At first, no one was sure where the shot had come from. Daisy managed to keep her gun concealed, but the soldiers closest decided not to take any chances and raised their weapons.

Zephyr took this moment to roar as loudly as he could and dive for the front car. Knowing what he intended to do, I clung to his back and concentrated on forming a moving barrier of air that went with us and ahead.

The soldiers spun the two artillery guns in our direction, but before either could fire, I blasted both sets of ammo with air, yanking the belts in a direction that instantly jammed one gun and a moment later jammed the other too. Something blew up in the face of an operator, making him yell.

By the time I'd done that, Zephyr was almost at ground level and he swooped over the first car, grabbing it in his claws with a screech of metal and hurling it like a bowling ball of death.

Some of the men tried to throw themselves out of the way. I held a barrier around us. Bullets pinged off Zephyr's scales here and there despite my best efforts, but I'd managed to deflect most of them, and I knew each bullet I stopped meant less pain for him.

As he wheeled away from the fire, Minsheng the team added to the fray, hurling fire and darts of their own. They took out a few more soldiers and agents who didn't know where to turn and were still scrambling to find cover.

I feared for my friends' lives against so much firepower, but I was so exhausted and spent that I couldn't protect them and Zephyr too. The large bronze dragon didn't hesitate; he came back over the convoy to grab another vehicle and hurl it at more soldiers.

Again the people beneath us scattered, but another couple of bullets tore through Zephyr's wings, and I heard him grunt in pain. I bit my lip since I felt the pain as well, but there was little I could do.

As we swept away for the second time, I noticed the soldiers had almost fixed the artillery and had moved both guns so they were positioned in front of some large trees for shelter. We were in big trouble if they got them up and running again. I wouldn't be able to attack them in the same way.

I was about to warn Zephyr when I heard a battle horn, and out of the forest on the other side of the road came an array of mythicals led by Lorcan. They paused on the tree line, using the silent sentinels for cover and firing guns they must have acquired from the agents and basic weapons like arrows of their own.

With the artillery still not working, they didn't come under as much fire, but I knew many of them were vulnerable to bullets in a way they wouldn't be expecting. Then I saw the four elven masters and Gwaelon as well. An elemental storm came down on the remaining soldiers and the bullets failed to reach their targets, blasted off course by water and air. Then the trees came to life and wrapped vines and branches around the soldiers or showered them in pine cones and nuts, keeping them busy and distracted.

Fire hit vehicles, igniting them on contact.

Without me needing to suggest it, Zephyr swept down again and exhaled, more gas rippling over the soldiers. This time it caught alight, enough fires blazing around the battleground that it became a burst of heated fumes within a moment. I followed it with attacks of my own since most of the agents and soldiers were now firing at other targets.

Attacked on two sides and with us in the air, the fifty or so men and women left put up the best fight they could. The elven masters soon waned in power, however. The fire and tree-based projectiles began to die down, and the air and water being used as barriers started to let projectiles through.

When the first artillery gun came back online again, the problem grew even worse.

Hang back, I told Zephyr, dropping the barrier I held around us to blast air at the jet of bullets from the first artillery gun as a centaur was cut down in a rain of shot.

I growled my frustration at them killing one of the

mythicals under my protection, but no matter how much I tried to force air at the stream of bullets, I could do little more than deflect and slow them, and it was quickly draining me.

The earth elementals must have realized the threat because a large tree reached out a branch and smacked the soldier who had been firing away. The bullets stopped long enough for several vines to wrap around the gun again and again.

I barely had a moment's reprieve before the second artillery gun was working. I blasted air at it, still sitting on Zephyr's back and far enough from the battle I was relatively safe.

As the vines and trees dealt with the other, however, I knew my tactic wasn't going to save anyone long-term.

I saw the earth master wobble, caught by the centaur behind him, the vines squeezing hard enough to break the first artillery gun into pieces.

Far to my right, Minsheng and Daisy had taken out several more soldiers, but blood dripped down Seth's arm, and Dyneira was running around on three legs.

Unless I could take out the second artillery gun, this battle was going to turn against us, and we were all going to die. The only effective strategy had been brought on by the earth elementals.

Thinking back to the little plant in my bag, I imagined that growing, then I imagined what I wanted to happen to the vines ahead of me, desperately hoping to see what I imagined. Nothing happened, but I wasn't about to give up while the elves needed me.

Could I and the earth elementals left standing do it together?

They linked arms, some of the younger elves who had been in the training square and even the master trying to stand with them, but the vines only crept slowly toward the second weapon.

I realized I could feel them doing it before I could see it, and then Zephyr swooped down.

What are you doing? I asked.

Landing so you can help them control those plants.

But—

You're already doing it, Aella, Zephyr yelled in my head. *You're making those plants grow. Get down there and join with them, and we might stand a chance.*

Zephyr landed between the artillery fire and its targets and roared, once again acting as a shield.

I slid down his back and ran to the elves who were trying to control the vines. Unable to concentrate on both my blast of air at the spray of bullets and control the vegetation, I dropped the former.

Immediately the bullets pounded into Zephyr's scales, the sound deafening.

The pain he felt exploded in my shoulder and chest, but he roared again and began to hurl anything he could get his claws on at anything that moved in front of him. The air and water elves with us redoubled their efforts to try to protect all of us, slowing some of the bullets and dulling the pain.

It was enough of a relief that I could concentrate once more. Linking my arm with the earth master and the nearest student of the same element, I gritted my teeth and pushed for control of the vines.

They sprang forward and wrapped around the artillery gun, yanking it out of the soldier's hand while flinging the man against the tree.

Unable to see it but somehow able to feel it, I focused along with the others on wrapping the vines and plants around it again and again and squeezing.

At first it resisted and a different kind of pain flared in my head, this one the usual pain I got when I was pushing my abilities too hard, but I ignored it and pushed even harder. Elves swayed in the line, but others came to support and help us for a moment. Suddenly the metal gave, the first give in the structure making the next bit easier until the weapon was useless.

Panting, I let the plant go and almost collapsed, my legs jelly and my body shaking. The pounding in my skull was clearly two-fold, partially from the pain Zephyr was experiencing while taking the bullets meant for us and partially from the way I'd pushed myself.

I tried not to think about what I'd just done or how and instead focused on the battle. We'd taken out the artillery, but we still had a lot of soldiers and agents fighting on.

Hurrying back to Zephyr, I threw up another barrier in front of him with the last bit of control I had, taking the sting out of more bullets and enabling him to march forward. He waded into battle, keeping his wings tucked up tight to protect them and lashing out with claws and fangs.

Someone thrust a gun at me, so I walked to his side, shooting anything that moved. It gave me a window. It was only as I hit the third person and they went down that I registered that I was using a real gun. At some point, my desire to fight back and protect and my anger and pain at being targeted because of my race had taken away my objections.

The soldiers were showing no mercy, and for now, I was giving them none.

With most of the elves spent and my abilities so drained I could barely keep my barrier up, I was expecting to be massacred at any moment. But the soldiers' numbers were so few that there was a ripple of surrender until everyone still standing had dropped their guns and placed their hands behind their heads. The rest were severely injured, unconscious, or dead.

Lorcan took over, getting mythicals to tend the wounded on both sides, restrain those who'd raised the white flag or were unconscious, and move some of the wreckage.

It was only after I'd stood in the middle of the road for several minutes, leaning against Zephyr, both of us panting and exhausted, that I realized that was where I was.

The road had become a battlefield, my only thoughts of the combatants and then relief that it was over. Thankfully, so late at night on such a quiet stretch of road, no cars had come, but we got lucky in that regard. Civilians getting hurt would have been another level of awful. As it was, I was still struggling to process that I'd just killed or at least severely injured people.

Around me, the mythicals grieved their dead and tended their wounded, and I knew this couldn't keep happening. Each time we clashed with the agency, more people got hurt and more people died. Something had to be done to keep the mythicals safe.

As I recovered and Zephyr nudged me with his head, I looked into his eyes. There were many dull aches on my body, and I was pretty sure there were plenty on him too.

You going to be okay? I asked when he limped toward the side of the road.

I hurt all over, but it's just bruising and muscle ache. Nothing got through the scales.

You have no idea how grateful I am that you're bulletproof, I replied, placing my hand on his side. It seemed right that there was physical contact between us after all this. I wanted to know he was there.

We wandered over to Minsheng, Ronan, and Lorcan. Minsheng wrapped me in a hug, and Ronan and Lorcan bowed.

"Once again, we are in your debt," Lorcan said before Ronan could.

"I only wish I could have saved everyone," I said, the tears that suddenly sprung out of my eyes choking off the last word.

Daisy came running up and hugged me too, and I cried. We had not managed to keep everyone alive. Not the mythicals, and not the agents and soldiers either.

When I next looked up, Zephyr's body was curled around me and Daisy, and I was pretty sure I saw moisture on his scales. Many of the others had joined us, including several of the elven masters. They looked as exhausted as I felt.

"I know you probably just want to rest and recover,"

Ruehnar said, "but we humbly request that you do so at the Sanctuary tonight."

I looked at Minsheng, my thoughts turning back to the dojo and warehouse. Even if they were safe, they would be worried about us.

"I've started getting everyone else ready to head back to the warehouse," Minsheng said as if he could read my mind. "We'll let them know you're fine and make sure nothing untoward is happening there."

"Now that the Sanctuary is safe once more, I will return to the dojo as well, if you'll have me again?" Ronan asked.

"You'll always be welcome," I replied instantly. "All mythicals are always welcome."

I noticed Seth lingering near the back of the group and hoped he'd heard my words. Even if I didn't like him, I wanted him to know he would find safety and respect anywhere I was in charge. He sported a bandage on his shoulder but otherwise looked his usual surly self.

He wasn't the only person lingering in the background. I noticed Agent Crawley and her daughter hanging back. Trying to ignore my aches and pains, I went over to them.

"Before either of you says anything, I'm not sure it would be safe for you to return to your normal lives. You're both welcome at the warehouse as well. It doesn't have to be permanent, but until you figure out what you do want to do, it's probably safest."

"Could I learn from you?" Emily asked immediately.

I nodded without hesitation. This young part-elven woman wasn't too dissimilar to me. She'd believed herself to be human and then found out she wasn't. The agency had then hunted her for it.

Although I had no idea what exactly she'd been through since then, I knew she needed a safe place to explore who she was and what that meant. I could give her what Minsheng had once given me.

She hugged me without warning, making me wince. Then Crawley came forward and encouraged Emily to help with the cleanup so we could all leave.

As her daughter hurried over to help Daisy with a task, Crawley looked at me.

"Thank you," she said. "For a moment there, I thought we were all going to die anyway. That my girl would never get to see a world where she was accepted. But you somehow always have another level of power, another way of dealing with those who've hurt you. People keep underestimating you, and they really shouldn't."

"Well, you know that now," I replied, not sure where this was going. She'd been the enemy once, but she'd been kinder than most.

"If you'll have me, I'd like to help you. It's clear I let fear dictate my actions before. I don't want to make that mistake in the future."

I nodded gratefully. I didn't think this clash with Jacobs was over. It was probably just beginning, but Crawley had information the others didn't and insight into his mind. Having her on my side would be a huge bonus after the fight we'd had this night. It gave me more peace of mind than I'd realized I'd needed.

"We should get going," Minsheng said, reaching out an arm to support me as I felt my body grow weaker. I was spent. "You need to rest."

Before long, the broken cars were all cleared to the

verge and people were packed into the working vehicles. Zephyr helped me onto the top of a tank and then climbed up. It groaned under his weight and couldn't move as fast, but neither of us had the energy to fly.

At some point, someone had handed me hot soup in a polystyrene cup and I slowly sipped it while I leaned against Zephyr, his tail curled around me and over my lap.

As I sat next to him, I looked at his scales, noticing they were discolored, shining in a multitude of colors like oil in a puddle. Was this what bruising looked like on a dragon?

Our tank was driven by Gwaelon, demonstrating that he was as versatile as he seemed. It made me wonder if he'd been the friend who'd found our first military vehicle.

Sleep, Zephyr said. *I'll keep you safe.*

What about you?

I can sleep while you talk to all these mythicals about what happens next, he replied, letting out a deep rumble of a chuckle.

Sounds like a plan. And then we'll get pizza.

I thought you'd forgotten.

Never, I replied, grinning at the mock-offense he'd spoken with.

My world was right again. We were together, safe enough, and once again joking about food.

CHAPTER TWENTY-FIVE

Cheering woke me up. Our vehicles were rolling into the streets of the Sanctuary, and the mythicals who had remained behind were out in force to welcome us home.

The sky had brightened, but the sun still hadn't appeared yet. I tried to move but instantly wished I hadn't. Pain flared everywhere at once.

Remind me to ask the next set of agents to go easier on us, I said to Zephyr. He chuckled but groaned as well as he tried to stretch. No doubt he hurt as much as I did. We needed to rest some as soon as people finished talking to us.

Part of me was angry that it couldn't seem to wait, but I knew there were plenty of people who were worried, had lost loved ones, or needed to plan to protect who was left. This couldn't wait, as much as I wanted it to.

Eventually our transport came to a stop, and Zephyr and I had little choice but to get down. The rest and food had made us strong enough to walk through yet another Sanctuary.

The new area they'd built in was on the edge of the

mountains, and it was as much in harmony with the surroundings as the previous cities. Its buildings were all hewn stone, natural arches of rock forming doorways and windows, and moss, lichens, and stocky bushes in the ornamental areas.

Yet again, it was beautiful, and I found myself in awe of the talents of the elves who'd constructed it.

As we were escorted to the new council chamber, I noticed it wasn't finished yet, most of the earth elemental elves having joined the battle. I could see what they were attempting, however.

They'd placed it in the center of the city, as always. This time, instead of being built upward, it was built into the mountain. An extremely large cave opening was adorned with plants and lit from within by warm, flickering lights.

The ground was soft underfoot, and for the first time, it was large enough for Zephyr. I walked close to him, Lorcan on my other side, and came to what looked like a large breakfast picnic, the council already fully convened.

As soon as they saw us, Vestan got up and rushed forward.

"We heard that your victory came at a high cost, but we had no idea how high. Come, sit, rest, and eat to regain your strength."

Relief at his warmth and concern almost made me tear up again, but instead, I let Vestan take my arm and guide both Zephyr and me to the seats clearly meant for us.

Zephyr and I were soon eating, the trusted warriors who'd fought at our sides also with us. While I ate, Lorcan informed the council of his part in the events, some of the timeline new to my ears. Ronan had contacted Lorcan as he'd said he would, but it had been Sierrathen who had insisted they send out an army once they understood our plan.

I listened until it became clear that I was expected to talk, and then I informed the council of everything else that had happened. I left out a few details. They didn't need to know who came and fought for me, nor that the mythical we'd found was the daughter of an agent who'd since pledged herself to my cause. Who I trusted was my concern.

They listened respectfully until we all talked about the final battle. Here the earth master chimed in.

"Aella turned the tide once more, controlling the plants along with us to great effect."

There were gasps, and I exhaled as every set of eyes fixed on me. Of course, none of the people who were at the battle were surprised. They'd seen what I'd done, even if they hadn't understood it.

"One of the first times I joined your elven masters as they taught in your Sanctuary, they told me I was clearly descended from the great elves of old. I had those beliefs confirmed by the organization. Your water master suggested that I might gain the abilities of more than one element."

"We thought that wasn't possible," Sierrathen replied.

"It may not have been," I said with a shrug, "but I can now use both air and earth, so it is theory no longer. I don't know if I can control all four elements, but I can control two at the moment."

"This is an interesting development, and I'm sure everyone elven has great interest in it," Vestan said. "However, we should get back to the matter of the Sanctuary's safety. Am I to understand that these agents can no longer use our orbs to find us?"

"Not currently," I replied and reiterated that we had rescued the mythical Jacobs had imprisoned.

There were murmurs and it was clear the Sanctuary council felt better about this, but not everyone looked pleased.

A lot of the orbs were destroyed or taken, Zephyr pointed out. *It's now very hard for mythicals out there to find the Sanctuary.*

You think this is why they're still tense?

The only alternative for mythicals seeking safety now is you, and some of them have made it clear that they think their way of life, hiding, is better.

They're not necessarily wrong, I replied as I thought about the situation and if there was anything I could do to help.

"Once we have rested, Zephyr and I will be happy to aid you in hiding new orbs and helping to ensure the fresh batch aren't taken, as we have previously offered," I said when it was clear no one else was going to speak and many were still staring at me.

"That would be helpful, I'm sure," Vestan replied.

"And I'm also willing to work with the elven masters in the city to understand the source of my dual elements." As I said these last words, I got up. While it had been helpful to break up my journey home and eat some more, we'd said everything I had any interest in saying, and I wanted to get back to the dojo and check that the rest of my friends were fine.

We also need pizza, Zephyr reminded me. I had to stifle a laugh.

"You would be most welcome, Aella and Zephyr," the earth master said, getting up and bowing as I was already doing toward Lorcan.

Nothing and no one prevented us from walking out of the council chambers except the aches and pains we bore. After picking up the belongings I'd left at the Sanctuary, including the plant I was growing, we got on the road, our party now far smaller.

As we neared LA, I wanted to hide instead to ride on top of a vehicle, but Zephyr didn't feel up to flying, and I wasn't going to leave his side. Instead, we waved at people and smiled to show how friendly we could be. For the most part it worked, but not everyone reacted favorably toward us.

I sighed, grateful when the dojo came into view. For a moment we did fly, heading up to the roof and in via the top. We were met with squeals of delight as I dropped my bag, then we made our way down to the kitchen and somewhere we could rest.

Minsheng and most of the others had been back for a while and had clearly told our friends everything, but Lyra insisted on hearing it all from me again.

After I'd told the story another couple of times, they allowed Zephyr and me to get some rest. We'd been up all night and had not slept much the nights before that. We'd almost become nocturnal with all the nighttime activity we'd gotten up to and the amount we'd slept during the day, but I didn't care. We would operate when we needed to for the safety of the dojo and the Sanctuary.

Once I was alone with Zephyr, we curled up, but I still couldn't sleep. While everyone else was now taking it for granted that I could control earth elements, I wasn't convinced. I'd done it in the heat of battle while linked to other elves. I had a feeling I'd only managed it because I'd had help. There was only one way to test that fear, however.

Hoping Zephyr wouldn't object to yet another thing delaying our sleep, I fetched the small plant I'd been carrying around with me and tried to concentrate. Zephyr shifted, bringing his head closer to mine.

You can do this, he said, his deep voice comforting. *I know you can. Just think about the memory of it working and what you want to happen now.*

At first nothing happened, but I tried to remember what it felt like as Zephyr had suggested, and then imagined my tiny sprout of a plant getting bigger. Again, nothing seemed to happen, but eventually, I realized it was growing. The progress was barely visible, but I was controlling the plant and encouraging it to grow.

Knowing I had a very smug grin on my face, I put the pot where it would get some sun at the beginning of each day and went back to Zephyr's side.

Do you ever get the feeling that there's a lot more to come in our lives? I asked Zephyr once we were comfortable and curled up together again.

All the time. But we'll face it together and one day at a time, so I don't usually worry about it.

I sighed. It was a good philosophy, and hearing it helped me relax. We'd worry about tomorrow when we woke up.

EPILOGUE

I laughed as Zephyr chowed down on yet more pizza. It was only a couple of days since we'd gotten back to the dojo, but we already felt loads better.

I'd considered what Jacobs might be up to a couple of times, and Ronan kept checking in with Lorcan to make sure the Sanctuary was now safe, but there had been no news to report. That was more than a little relieving.

When Zephyr finished eating and burped, I rolled my eyes. Justin, Tristan, and Grim were also in the room, along with Katrina, their sphinx. No sooner had they gotten up and taken the plates to the sink than Chris came running in.

"Minsheng says you're going to want to see the news he has," Chris said before hurrying back the way he'd come.

Worry making my shoulders tense, I got to my feet and hurried after him, aware Zephyr was following me even though I couldn't see or hear him doing so.

We made our way up to the next floor. It was partway through preparations to be built upon, the organization showing they had friends in high places by getting the planning approved and funding the construction costs to add a floor of bedrooms and recreational space as well as a new roof terrace on top of that.

My eyes went to the screen Minsheng was staring at. A reporter stood beside the forest where we'd fought the agents a couple of days ago. When he noticed we'd joined him, Minsheng turned the sound up but didn't look away.

"It's clear that a lot of damage was done here and many people fought on both sides of what must have been a very nasty and brutal attack," the reporter said.

I gulped. This didn't sound good.

The camera panned the wreckage and the damage to the road and forest. Amongst it were more than a few bloodstains and broken pieces of vehicle or weapons, including the two artillery guns wrapped in vines.

Before I could ask what had been said earlier, the shot cut back to the studio. A man sat with another reporter, the caption at the bottom declaring him to be none other than the Jacobs we'd been targeted by, his voice easily recognizable.

Shitsticks, I thought, knowing where this was likely to go next. Jacobs opened his mouth to continue the conversation they'd been having.

"As you can see, the convoy was attacked by mythicals who could control the elements. Fire, the forest itself, and an arsenal of weaponry we cannot easily defend against. They massacred the soldiers and agents who were part of that convoy. There was no warning. They'd pulled over because of a flat tire on an important vehicle and were forced to defend themselves."

"Was there no warning at all?"

"None. Just an attack."

I frowned and swore some more. He was painting us as brutal killers, and I could do nothing but watch.

They talked for a little longer about what had happened, the man making it sound worse and worse until the reporter decided to take a different tack.

"I understand you are working with the US government to try to ensure this doesn't happen again."

"Yes. It's clear that no one is policing these mythicals, as they like to call themselves. We're looking to set up a branch of the government that does so in much the same way we have the ATF and the FBI for different matters that span multiple states."

"Shitsticks," I said aloud. "He wants to save the agency and become our law enforcement."

"It's an effective move." Chris walked closer, his comment showing that he'd heard the whole thing.

"Over my dead body," I replied. "No one is going to start arresting mythicals on jumped-up charges without going through me first."

"I was hoping you'd say that," Minsheng said, a light appearing in his eyes. "I might have an idea."

The story continues with *Night Sworn*, book 5 in the
Dragon of Shadow and Air series.

Claim your copy today!

ACKNOWLEDGMENTS

Another massive thank you to everyone at LMBPN for making another book in the series happen. I love these characters so much and you help get them out there to readers who love them just as much. I really can't express my gratitude enough.

To Ella for yet more editing genius. You always make the stories and characters I write so much better than they could be otherwise. And you keep me on my toes and learning even after a decade of practice.

To Anne for my book dragon who keeps me company while I write these stories.

To Bear, for always being supportive and not minding when I plot spoil and tell you things in latter books to get my head around them and simply make sure I'm not the only person who knows.

To Phil for putting up with the chaos that's in my head and for not minding when I'm not always 'there'.

To the tiny humans, for reminding me that sometimes

it takes a hundred attempts for someone to learn something and sometimes it just clicks and you get it first time.

And to God, for knowing what's in my heart.

ABOUT THE AUTHOR

Jess was born in the quaint village of Woodbridge in the UK, has spent some of her childhood in the States and now resides near the beautiful Roman city of Bath. She lives with her husband, Phil, her two tiny humans (one boy and one girl) and her very dapsy cat, Pleaides.

During her still relatively short life Jess has displayed an innate curiosity for learning new things and has therefore studied many subjects, from maths and the sciences, to history and drama. Jess now works full time as a writer and mummy, incorporating many of the subjects she has an interest in within her plots and characters.

When she's not busy with work and keeping her tiny humans alive she can often be found with friends, playing with miniature characters, dice and pieces of paper covered in funny stats and notes about fictional adventures her figures have been on.

You can find out more about the author and her upcoming projects by joining her on facebook, by watching her live D&D streams, or emailing her via books@jessmountifield.co.uk. Jess loves hearing from a happy fan so please do get in touch!

Jess is also opening up her discord for fans to come chat about what she's up to, and see a few sneak peaks of future work. There's also a chance to become one of her beta readers. If you'd like to check that out you can do so <u>here.</u>

CONNECT WITH JESS

Connect with Jess Mountifield

Mailing list sign up
Facebook group.
Discord group
Actual play D&D stream: Twitch or Youtube
Email address: contact me here.

BOOKS BY JESS MOUNTIFIELD

Already published

Urban Fantasy

Dragon of Shadow and Air:

Air Bound

Shadow Sworn

Dragon Souled

Earth Bound

Night Sworn (Coming soon)

Fantasy

Tales of Ethanar:

Wandering to Belong (Tale 1)

Innocent Hearts (Tale 2 & 3)

For Such a Time as This (Tale 4)

A Fire's Sacrifice (Tale 5)

Winter Series:

The Hope of Winter (Tale 6.05)

The Fire of Winter (Tale 6.1)

Guild of the Eternal Flame:

Wayfarer's Sanctuary

Protector's Secret

Healer's Oath

Other Fantasy:

The Initiate (under Holly Lujah)

Writing with Dawn Chapman:

Jessica's Challenge (#5 in the Puatera Online series)

Dahlia's Shadow (#6 in the Puatera Online series)

Lila's Revenge (#7 in the Puatera Online series)

Sci-Fi:

Fringe Colonies:

Alliance

Haven

Rebellion

Rebirth

Reclamation

Star Trail:

Hunted

Sherdan series:

Sherdan's Prophecy

Sherdan's Legacy

Sherdan's Country

Sherdan's Road (A short story in the anthology 'The End of the Road')

The Slave Who'd Never Been Kissed (A short in the charity anthology 'Imaginings')

New Beginnings

Santa's Little Space Pirate

In the multi-author Adamanta series:

Episode 1 – Adamanta

Episode 3 – Excelsior

Episode 8 – Phoenix

Episode 13 – New Contacts

Episode 17 – Sacrifice

Other:

Clues, Claws and Christmas

Non-Fic:

How to Write Lots, and Get Sh*t Done: the Art of Not Being a Flake

Find purchase links here

Coming soon:

Urban Fantasy:

Dragon of Shadow and Air:

Dryad Souled

Water Bound

Day Sworn

Fantasy

(Tales of Ethanar):

The Pursuit of Winter (#2 in the Winter series, Tale 6.2)

Books under Amelia Price

Mycroft Holmes Adventures:

The Hundred Year Wait

The Unexpected Coincidence

The Invisible Amateur

The Female Charm

The Reluctant Knight

The Ambitious Orphan

The Unconventional Honeymoon Gift

The Family Reunion

The Immortal Problem

Coming soon:

The Unremarkable Assistant

OTHER BOOKS FROM LMBPN PUBLISHING

Sign up for the LMBPN email list to be notified of new releases and special deals!

https://lmbpn.com/email/

For a complete list of books by LMBPN please visit:

https://lmbpn.com/books-by-lmbpn-publishing/